The Blackmail Photos

The Travelers: Book 3

Michael P. King

Blurred Lines Press

Blurred Lines Press
The Blackmail Photos
Michael P. King
ISBN 978-0-9861796-5-5

Cover design by Paramita Bhattacharjee at
creativeparamita.com

The Blackmail Photos is a work of fiction. The names, characters, places, and events are products of the author's imagination.

"In this third installment of his Travelers series, King's (*The Computer Heist*, 2016, etc.) con-artist couple target a would-be politician. . . . As usual, King's dialogue and secondary characters make for rich, pulpy reading; . . . he masterfully crafts the deadly tangle of interpersonal alliances and their fallout. . . . A tightly executed thriller, and the high point of a great series."—*Kirkus Reviews*

Blackmail. Deceit. Revenge. The Travelers, going by the names George and Roslyn Harrison, entrap a congressional candidate with photos of his extramarital affair. But just as George is hatching a ploy to increase their ill-gotten gains, the candidate's wife uncovers the plot. With their scheme careening sideways and the sheriff closing in, Roslyn receives news that drastically alters the scope of their plan. Is this a golden opportunity or a horrible misstep?

The Blackmail Photos is a noir crime thriller that will keep you turning pages until the very end. If you like fast-paced action, surprising plot twists, and criminal shenanigans, then you'll love the third installment of Michael P. King's Travelers series.

For Sarah, forever, all my love.

1: The Setup

The last week in January, the Traveling Man, a con man currently going by the name George Harrison, sat in a gray panel
van parked across the street from a yellow-brick, ranch-style
house with a two-car garage and a real estate agent's FOR SALE
sign sticking up out of the snow in the front yard. The van's
engine was turned off. The driver's window was cracked a
couple of inches to keep the inside of the windows from frosting
up. George had dark hair speckled with gray and a nose slightly
broken to the right. He wore insulated blue coveralls with a
cable company logo on the back, insulated work boots, and a
black stocking cap, but he was still cold. Thirty minutes ago,
he'd been in the ranch to turn on the heat. Now all he could do
was wait and curse the cold. It was late afternoon and almost
dark; the streetlights had just come on. He hoped the waiting
would be worth it. He'd completed his part of the prep; now it
was up to his wife, currently going by the name Roslyn. A tan
minivan drove by and turned into a nearby driveway. A little
girl in a light-purple parka jumped out of the side door dragging a pink backpack through the snow behind her and ran up
the front steps. The minivan backed into the street, kissing the
side of the snow pile by the driveway. George dropped down in
his seat until it had rolled by.

From down in the seat, he could see headlights in his side
mirror. The door rose on the ranch's two-car garage. A red
Lincoln MKS, followed by a white Cadillac STS, pulled into the
garage. The garage door closed. George climbed into the back of
the van, picked up a tool bag appropriate to a cable repair

1

technician, and climbed out the back doors. He stood for a moment and watched the lights come on in the house as Roslyn — red Lincoln — and Donald Honeycutt — white Cadillac — moved from the garage, through the kitchen and living room, to the bedrooms. He adjusted his cap and rubbed his three-day beard. Time to get moving. He looked both ways before he crossed the street. Dead quiet. The snow reflected the light from the streetlamps and the porch lights of the houses, giving the twilight a soft glow. He walked up the driveway and then marched through the snow around to the back of the house, just as if he'd been doing this all day. The backyard of the house was all darkness and long shadows. A tall wooden fence blocked the view and no dogs barked. That's why he and his wife had chosen this house. When he reached the master bedroom, he crouched under the window at the spot where Roslyn had left a slit in the drapes.

He could see everything. She hadn't wasted any time. She and Honeycutt were already lying on the red blanket in the empty room, his wife's thin, athletic body intertwined with Honeycutt's large, soft form: their lips locked together, their hands groping each other as they moved rhythmically together. George took the digital camera out of his tech bag, selected Video Recording, and then filmed them until they stood up, and his wife turned Honeycutt so that George could get the full-frontal shot. She was certainly playing at the top of her game today. He turned off the camera, slipped it back in the bag, and tried to walk in his own footsteps back around the house. As he trudged back down the driveway, a steel-blue Honda minivan drove past. The woman behind the wheel gave him a hard look. He waved like he'd be at her house next. No worries. The cable would be fixed before tonight's shows came on. He crossed the street and climbed into the panel van. Finally, he could go home and warm up. It was all up to Roslyn now, and she was the kind of closer who didn't take no for an answer.

Roslyn and Honeycutt stood in the center of the empty room — she in her lacy white panties, he in his baby-blue boxers. She had one hand on his hip and the other on his chest. He was slightly over six feet tall, baby-faced, with curly red hair and light-blue eyes that always seemed to be smiling. She looked up into his face, stood up on her tiptoes, and kissed him. "I love you," she said. She tossed her head as she stepped down onto her heels, her reddish-brown hair dancing around her shoulders.

He grabbed her hands. "You know, even though I told you how things had to be right from the beginning, I think maybe I love you, too."

She pouted, stepped away to her clothing laid out on the carpet near the door, slipped on her bra, and turned her back to him as she fastened it. "Don't get my hopes up, Donny, if you don't mean it. This isn't a joke to me."

He followed after her and took her in his arms from behind, crossing his hands to cup her breasts. "I know; I know. I can't promise you anything. I'm just telling you how I feel. I'm married. You're married. Neither one of us can afford to do anything crazy."

She squirmed around in his arms and laid her face against his chest. "Then let's not do anything crazy. The time we're together is too special for us to ruin it."

He kissed her. "I don't know how I found you."

"Me too."

He looked at his watch behind her back. "I'm late."

She smiled. "Again?"

"Easy for you to laugh."

"What time is it?"

"Quarter to six."

"I'm late, too."

Out in the garage, they stood in their suits and overcoats and kissed one last time between the cars. "When will I see you again?" she asked.

"I'll text you from my burner."

"I've got some open time tomorrow."

"I'm jammed up tomorrow. Maybe I could see you late, though, if you could slip away."

"Okay."

"I've got to go." He got into his white Cadillac. She raised the garage door and watched him back into the street, his taillights casting a red shadow on the snow.

3

Then she got into her Lincoln, started it, and got the heat and the heated seats going before she took out her phone. "Hey, baby. It's all good."

"Excellent," George said.

"How about your end?"

"Come see for yourself."

"I'm on my way."

"I'm waiting for you, honey."

Honeycutt walked into his campaign office, a storefront one block off the city square in downtown Randal Junction. The poster in the window, trimmed in red and blue, said, "HONEYCUTT—FOR A FRESH START." The door was open, but there was no one in the main room. Four dented gray metal desks matched with discount-store office chairs, a stack of green metal folding chairs against the far wall, industrial fluorescent lights, and dusty off-white walls in need of a fresh coat of paint: it was hard even for Honeycutt to believe a person could become a member of the US House of Representatives starting from here. He heard a voice and saw Evelyn Wall, his campaign manager, through the picture window into the back office. She was walking back and forth in front of her old oak desk as she talked on the phone. She wore a black sports coat with a calf-length blue skirt. Her gray-brown hair was braided down her back, and her frameless glasses hung on a gold chain from her neck. She looked up, smiled, and motioned for him to come back.

He pantomimed, "Where is everyone?"

She rolled her eyes, said "Good-bye," and hung up the phone. "The college kids all thought you blew them off."

"I'm not that late."

She took him by the shoulders and kissed his cheek. "Running for the US House is not like running for county commission. The interns are much more serious, for one thing. Toss your coat on that chair." She indicated an extra oak armchair that sat in the corner. "Sit."

She sat in the high-backed manager's chair behind her desk. He sat in the armchair facing her without taking off his overcoat.

4

"You need to up your game."

"I'm not a kid or a fool, Evelyn. So don't try to lecture me. I'm in this to win."

Evelyn nodded. "Have you spoken to your wife today?"

He shook his head.

"She rolled through here earlier. Met with the new volunteers. They're a good crew. They should be a big help as we ramp up. Anyway, we were talking about endorsements from popular politicians. It's a given that statewide officials are going to wait until after the primary, though Billie thinks the secretary of state might help behind the scenes because of the help she and Tommy gave him when he was starting out."

"Wouldn't hold my breath."

"That's what I told her." She picked up a pencil off her desk and started scratching on a notepad. "We know we can count on the sheriff—he doesn't like you, but he doesn't hate you, and he's Billie's ex-brother-in-law. The mayor endorsed the sheriff, but we found out today that his cousin is working for Kate Blackthorne's campaign, so he's doubtful. Bottom line is, we need as many suburban and small town mayors, and county officials here and in Gilbert and Pender Counties as we can get."

Honeycutt nodded. "I agree. At least we've already got the banks and developers on our side."

"Most of them."

He shrugged. "The ones that count. Anyway, some of them ought to be able to help us with city and county officials."

"Less than five months until the primary."

"It'll go by in the blink of an eye."

"That's what I'm afraid of."

He stood up. "Lock up and go home, Evelyn. We'll be ready when it's time. We'll crush Blackthorne, Melburn will drop out, and Deal never had a chance. It doesn't get tough until we face Daniels in the fall."

Roslyn walked up the front steps to her and George's apartment in the light cast from the porch lamp. She held her gray overcoat closed with one hand and kept a sharp eye out for ice. When she got to the door, George opened it. He folded her in

5

his arms before she could even shut the door or get her coat off. "I love you so much," he said.

"I need to take a shower."

"You smell fine just the way you are." He kissed her eyes and her nose and her mouth.

"Let me at least get out of the cold." He let go of her and shut the door. She hung up her overcoat in the front closet. Their apartment was a deluxe one-bedroom with an open floor plan chosen to support their cover as real estate agents. The living room/dining room had tan walls with white crown molding and five-inch baseboards. The kitchen had granite counters and stainless steel appliances. The rent-to-own furniture—a sofa with two matching chairs—was an understated paisley with a tan background. A big screen TV sat at the far end of the room.

"How's the video?"

"Come look."

They sat on the sofa next to each other and watched the video recording on the screen on the back of the camera. There she was with Honeycutt: missionary position, cowgirl, doggie style. "This is some of your best camera work."

"Come on, what really makes the film is when you turn him for the full frontal. There's no deniability there." He turned off the camera and set it on the coffee table. "Dying your hair to match his wife's—that was genius." He picked up her hand and kissed it. "The way you reeled him in. You should be giving lessons."

"He told me he loved me."

"He told you he loved you? Honey, you're outdoing yourself."

"He's just another horndog, baby, an overgrown boy who thinks he's God's gift to women. Easy pickings. What makes him special is that you don't find many horndogs who are bankers running for Congress."

George laughed. "You got that right. We were lucky to stumble over him."

"I'm going to shower."

"You hungry? We've got plenty of time before we hit the McMansion."

"We still going to do that now that Honeycutt is underway?"

"I know, I know, rule number one, no complications. But Honeycutt isn't making us any money yet, and the McMansion is too good to pass up."

She patted his leg. "Okay, let me shower and change. You up for Chinese?"

"That place downtown or out by the strip mall?"

She stood up. "Out at the strip mall they have the best eggrolls."

"You want a drink while you get ready?"

"I'm fine."

"I'm going to have a short one."

Three hours later they were parked in the gray panel van on the street in front of a massive two-story red brick house with a three-car garage in Riverview Heights, a large lot subdivision just outside the city limits of Randal Junction. The driveway and sidewalks had been scraped clean earlier that day by a snow removal company. The owners of the house were out of town for the week, the real estate company that George and Roslyn worked for was minding the store, and the alarm system—a simple interior door and window program with zoned motion detection—was woefully inadequate for such a remote location, even if George hadn't filched the access code at the office. Still, George had taken the time to put magnetized fake license plates over the real plates when they had picked up the van. "Ready?" George asked.

Roslyn nodded.

They got out of the van. They were wearing dark-colored cross-country ski clothes, the goggles set up on their knit caps, and throwaway latex gloves. The night was silent. The outside lights were off, but the first floor lights were on. They walked straight up to the front door. George picked the lock and pushed the door open. They pulled down their goggles, just in case there were surveillance cameras that they didn't know about. Roslyn rushed over to the alarm panel on the entryway wall, disarmed the alarm, and then waved back at George.

The entryway was two stories high, and the stairway was dark-stained maple. To the right was a dining room featuring a long walnut table, to the left was a huge living room centered on a giant, river-stone fireplace. They moved quickly up the stairs and down the hall to the master bedroom suite. The bedroom suite faced the back of the house, so George turned on the lights. The king-size bed was canopied with flower-embroidered gauze curtains, which matched the curtains on the bank of windows across the back of the room. Roslyn went into the woman's walk-in closet and searched the dresser drawers. No jewelry. No money. She felt through the hanging clothes — dresses, blouses, and skirts — and the handbags racked in the shelves. Nothing. She pulled down the boxes from the top shelf. Packing paper. She moved on to the bathroom.

Meanwhile, George went into the man's walk-in closet. Similarly, there was nothing of value in the dresser, or suit pockets, or on the top shelf. But behind a full-length mirror was a wall safe. "Honey," he yelled over his shoulder.

"Yeah?"

"Try behind the mirror."

"When I finish with the bath."

The safe was a simple, third-rate model that posed no challenge. Inside were personal papers and $5,000 in an envelope. He took the money and closed the safe. Roslyn met him in the bedroom. She shook her head. "Nothing in the bath and nothing behind the mirror."

He grinned, held up the envelope, and then stuffed it into his jacket. She turned off the light as they left the bedroom. Downstairs they separated; she took the dining room and kitchen back to the family room, while he moved through the living room. Nothing stood out. As an afterthought, they went down into the basement. She flipped on the lights. The walls were clean, unpainted concrete. A weight bench and an elliptical trainer stood in the center of the room. Unpainted wooden shelves on the wall at the far end were loaded with boxes marked with their contents: x-mas, office 1998, pictures scanned, tax records 2005–2010, 2011–2015. A door beside the shelves led to the furnace room. As they turned to go, they saw another door on the other side of the stairs. Through that door they found the wine cellar, a temperature-controlled space with what looked to be around two hundred bottles of wine racked around the walls. Bingo. George shook out a folded-up duffel bag, which they packed with wine labeled "ready to drink."

Back in the corner past the white wine, Roslyn noticed a large, black plastic toolbox. She flipped up the top. Inside were several jewelry-store boxes — she opened one and saw a ring — and two envelopes of money. She dumped the boxes and the envelopes into the duffel on top of the wine.

George nodded. "Time to leave."

He shouldered the bag with a grunt and trudged up the stairs. "Jesus. Should have been choosier." Once up the stairs, he dragged the duffel across the wood floor to the front door.

"Easy or hard?" Roslyn asked.

"We've been in the goodies, so we've got to throw them off track."

"It's a shame to fuck up such a nice place."

"Be a shame to go to jail." George went into the kitchen and started dumping the contents of the refrigerator out onto the brick-red tile floor, glass condiment jars breaking, fruits and vegetables bouncing and rolling. Roslyn opened the milk jug and threw the jug into the dining room, milk splashing over the floral wallpaper and dark oak floor. Then she opened the ketchup and stomped on it, shooting a spray of ketchup across the tan-gray family room carpet. George tossed her a can of Coke, which she opened and threw at the cream-colored family room sofa.

"Enough?"

George nodded. He pulled open the freezer, tossed the chocolate ice cream into the dining room, and left the freezer door open. "I'll pull the van up. Wait for me."

George left the front door open. Roslyn stood by the alarm controller in the front hall. George pulled the van up in the driveway without turning on the headlights, jumped out, and ran up the sidewalk and into the house, where he heaved up the duffel with both hands. "Okay."

He lugged the duffel back to the van, walking like a hunchback under the weight, and shoved it into the back. Roslyn reset the alarm, tripped it, and ran out to the van, leaving the lights on and the front door open. They drove one block without the headlights, and then turned them on and took a left out of Riverview Heights. The night was cold and still. A half-moon illuminated the back road they'd chosen to use as their escape route. George turned on his brights. Two deer meandered in the deep snow near the edge of the road. He slowed down, watching them, expecting them to jump into the road at the least convenient moment, but they turned toward an evergreen bush and disappeared. Two miles toward town, George pulled over and took off the magnetic license plates. They still hadn't heard any police sirens. He slipped the plates into a bag and set the bag beside the duffel in the back. "When we get back to the Shop-N-Save where we left the Avalon, we're wiping down this van and leaving it. Don't want to tempt fate."

It was 1:00 a.m. by the time they were safely back at their apartment. The wine was stacked in the pantry closet. An open bottle of red was on the kitchen counter, next to the cash and four open jewelry boxes, which contained an emerald ring, a pearl necklace, a woven gold bracelet, and a pair of matching gold earrings. George stood in the middle of the living room holding a glass of wine. "Twelve thousand plus the jewelry. Now we can really play it smart with Honeycutt."

Roslyn sat on the sofa with her bare feet up on the coffee table. "We going to follow the usual plan?"

"I'll edit the video, make a copy, and print a couple of stills to get him interested in looking at the DVD."

She sipped her wine. "I'm surprising I can still get away with it."

George cocked his head and gave her a quizzical look. "Honey, you are a beautiful woman. You look as good as you ever did, and you have the allure that comes from emotional maturity. You are irresistible to the middle-aged man."

"You really think so?"

He sat down beside her, took her glass from her hand, and took both her hands in his. "Roz, have you ever seen me carry a slacker on a job?"

"No."

"Then you know you have what it takes to do your part." He kissed her forehead. "And if I thought you weren't up to it anymore, or if you didn't want to do it anymore, we'd just put you to training and looking after a new girl. You've got too much experience, we've been together too long, and, besides, I love you. We're always going to be together."

10

Her eyes glistened. He took her in his arms and held her, rubbing her back and kissing her neck.

"Oh, Georgie," she whispered, "I don't deserve you."

"Yes, you do," he said. "Yes, you do."

2: The Photos

Two days later, Honeycutt and his wife, Billie Teardale Honeycutt, sat facing each other on padded stools at the black granite counter that separated their kitchen from their family room. The sun shined bright through the tall casement windows in the family room. The weather had warmed the last few days and the snow had melted off the low spots, revealing dead grass and fallen sticks. Honeycutt was wearing dark-blue pajamas. Reading glasses were perched on his nose, and his red hair was mussed from the bed. The morning newspaper sat on the stool next to his. Billie was wearing a mauve fleece robe over a one-quarter button white silk sleep shirt. Her reddish-brown hair, the gray carefully touched up, was tucked behind her ears. She already had on a little neutral-colored lipstick. Half a grapefruit with a spoon stuck in it sat in front of her. Mamie Peters, their elderly housekeeper, dressed in a black dress and white apron, her gray hair pulled back in a bun, was behind them in the kitchen. "You got a package yesterday evening, Mr. Donald."

"Mr. Donald," he muttered before he said, "Where is it?"

Mamie went out to the hall table where the mail accumulated.

Billie touched Honeycutt's hand. "You ought to know by now that she's not going to change her ways."

"I'm never going to get used to it."

"And she feels weird not saying mister and missus."

"But I'm the boss. She's supposed to accommodate me."

"Dream on."

Mamie handed Honeycutt a cardboard FedEx mailer. He pulled the tab and looked inside. He caught a view of Roslyn's breasts, closed the envelope a little too quickly, and set it on the newspaper.

Billie looked at him sharply. "You look like you've seen a ghost. What is it?"

"Nothing. Some silly banking business I didn't want to think about this early in the morning. Should have gone to the office."

"It's not something I can help you with?"

"No, no. Nothing for you to worry about. Nothing to do with the election."

Billie took a bite of grapefruit. Mamie poured her some fresh coffee. "No more for me," Honeycutt said.

"Mamie," Billie said, "have you found someone to help with the cleaning since Rosa left?"

"I can manage, ma'am."

"You will hire someone. You're like my mom to me. I won't have you overworked. And you're grumpy when you're tired. So hire someone or I'll do it for you."

She smiled. "Yes, ma'am." She put the coffee pot back into the coffee maker and left the room.

Honeycutt looked over his shoulder to make sure she was gone. "That little old lady should be in a home, not working here."

"She is in a home. My home. Come on, Donny, you know she's been with me almost twenty years."

"What about when she can't work anymore?"

"You don't have any idea of what goes on around here, do you? She can't work now. Juan takes care of the outside, Chrissie and whoever replaces Rosa take care of the inside, and Mamie very gently drives them all crazy."

"You're a saint."

"That's what I've been telling you."

"What's on your plate today?"

"Still hoping to sell that last piece of property out by the free-way, but I'm not willing to give it away, so I don't think Ricardo is going to bite."

"Patience. Maybe he'll start negotiating when he sees you're serious."

"And I'm going out to Tommy's grave. It's the ten-year anniversary."

He patted her hand. "I'm really sorry. I forgot all about it. You feeling okay?"

"Why should you remember? He wasn't your first husband."

"You free for lunch? I'll take you to Olive's Tea Room."

"That would be nice."

Honeycutt looked at the clock on the microwave. "I've got to get moving. I'll swing by to get you at noon."

"I'll already be in the car, so I'll come by the bank."

Honeycutt picked up the FedEx mailer, stepped around the end of the granite island to kiss Billie, and headed upstairs. He needed to see what was in the mailer. Good thing Billie hated to open mail. Whoever sent it must not care if she saw the picture. If the picture really was of Roslyn. Maybe his mind was playing tricks on him. He'd been feeling guilty ever since he'd told Roslyn that he loved her. That was foolish. And dishonest. His relationship with Billie was the only relationship that mattered, which was why she didn't care about his playmates, as long as he was discrete.

He went into his bathroom, shut the door, locked it, and then unlocked it. *Stop being paranoid. Get ready for the day.* He set the mailer on the counter, took off his pajama shirt, got out his shaving cream and razor, splashed warm water on his face, and put some shaving cream in his hand. He looked at himself in the mirror—winter white and freckles—stopped what he was doing, rinsed the shaving cream off of his hand, and toweled off his face. He had to know. He opened the mailer and pulled its contents out onto the counter. On top was an 8 × 11 photo of him and Roslyn having sex. It was an excellent picture. They were completely naked. He was lying on top of her. He was clasping her hands down over her head, and they were looking in each other's eyes. There was absolutely no doubt as to their identities. Under the photo was a DVD labeled "private" in black Sharpie and a note printed on plain paper. "Enjoy the DVD. The first of every month, $10,000 in cash goes into the mailbox listed below or your wife, the newspapers, the TV stations, and the Internet get this DVD. Do the right thing, congressman-elect."

14

Honeycutt crumpled the note and dropped it on the white tile floor. He was so screwed. What to do? What to do? He looked at the picture again, studying the background, but it was just a red sheet or blanket. There was nothing else in the picture except their naked bodies. He should tear up the picture and flush it down the toilet. Then Billie couldn't stumble upon it. He'd promised her he'd stay off the women until after the election. All he needed was her finding this picture on the anniversary of her perfect husband's accidental death. He flipped up the toilet lid and tore the picture in half. Wait. He needed to see Roslyn, show her the picture and the note, see how she reacted. Maybe this problem was still fixable. If it were all just Roslyn, he could get this problem cleared up in no time. Wouldn't be the first time a girlfriend had threatened to tell his wife. He picked up the note, smoothed it out, and put everything back in the mailer. He needed to focus. One, keep Billie from finding out. Two, find out who was behind this. What time was it? He pulled his smartphone from his pajama pants pocket. Seven thirty. Late enough to text Roslyn. He should use the burner out in his car, but he didn't want to wait. He keyed in her phone number. "Trouble. Meet behind campaign office. Eight thirty."

He shaved and dressed: he chose a charcoal suit, light-blue striped shirt, and silver tie. While he was tying his black wing-tips, his phone beeped. The message back from Roslyn said, "On my way." He walked across the master suite to Billie's bathroom and cracked open the door. The fan was running, the room was steamed up, and the shower was on. "I'm off."

"Have a good morning," Billie said from inside the shower.

"See you at noon."

Roslyn's red Lincoln was already parked between the rust-red Dumpsters behind the campaign office when Honeycutt drove up the alley. He squeezed in next to her Lincoln, blocking the gray steel door to the back of the office. She got out of her car and got into his Cadillac. She was wearing a silver-gray parka over a black pants suit with a red-green pattern scarf wrapped around her neck. "What's up?" she said.

He took the two halves of the photo out of the mailer and handed them to her. She held the two halves together. He watched her carefully. Her eyes darted over the picture. "What?

Where? Oh, my God." Her eyes flooded over, and tears started down her cheeks. "Where did this come from? George can't see this. Is this the only one?"

"It came with a DVD and a note."

She clutched the halves of the photo to her chest and started rocking in her seat. "Oh, no. Oh, no. Oh, no." She looked for his eyes. "George will kill me. I'll lose my job. What did the note say?"

"Ten thousand dollars a month or the DVD goes viral."

"You'll lose the election."

"I'd have to drop out."

"Probably wouldn't get reelected to the county commission."

"That's the least of it."

She set the photo down, got out a tissue, and dabbed her face.

"Have you looked at the DVD?"

He shook his head. "Opened the mailer this morning."

"What are you going to do?"

"Don't want Billie or Sheriff Teardale to know. Not yet, anyway. There's got to be some way to make this go away. I just don't know what it is yet, so I think I'm going to have to pay. At least for now."

"Are you sure? That's a lot of money."

He nodded. "And we're going to have to lay low for a while."

"What?"

"Can't be acting suspicious."

She put her face in her hands and turned away. "Did you just make all this up to get rid of me?"

"What? No." He put his hand on her shoulder. "You're overwrought. Calm down and think. We've got to play it safe. If we get caught, we really will be screwed. You get a burner and call my burner. Somebody knew where we were and filmed us. No meetings and no regular phones until we have a handle on this." He looked at his watch. "I've got to go."

She reached across the car and grabbed the front of his overcoat with both hands. Her voice broke as she spoke. "Don't forget about me."

He leaned forward and kissed her tenderly. "Go on. I'll be in touch."

He watched her rush back to her car. The way her emotions pulsed back and forth, there was no way she was involved. Afraid of her husband, questioning the cost, accusing him of ditching her — she wasn't thinking clearly at all. Had to be someone else. Someone who knew his schedule — or her schedule. Maybe he'd be able to see more background on the DVD. If he knew where the video was taken, maybe that would help him figure out who was behind it. He waved at Roslyn as she drove away. One thing for certain, it wasn't a political rival. Any of those weasels would have exposed him or threatened to expose him if he didn't drop out of the race. Maybe someone at her real estate office. Half of them were talented professionals; the other half were crooks hoping for a score. The stories Billie told about her dealings with real estate types. Jesus. He started his car and backed out into the alley. Someone had him by the short hairs. He'd be in their power until he could figure out who they were, get all the original material from them, and find a permanent way to shut them up. And somehow keep Billie in the dark. He was fucked. She would hit the roof if she found out. He wanted to go back to bed, wake up, and find out this whole situation was nothing but a bad dream. His phone vibrated. Message from Evelyn: meeting with mayor in one hour. Christ. It just never ended.

Honeycutt and Evelyn sat on the cream-colored sofa in the far corner of Mayor Frank Ketchum's office in the rehabbed railway station that served as city hall. The mayor sat across from them on a matching chair. A silver coffee service sat on the table between them. A row of old-fashioned double-hung windows ran across the outside wall, which faced the 1920s brown brick façade of the First National Bank across the street. The windows were covered by shear curtains and outlined by heavy drapes in a cream, burgundy, and green stripe. Nearer to the door was the mayor's massive oak desk, a lawyer's desk, flanked by two matching oak armchairs. The mayor had to lean forward in his chair to keep his feet on the carpet, which made his belly hang over his belt. The light shone through the brown hair combed over the top of his head, and his moustache was a little long around the edges of his mouth, but he still managed to seem serious and important.

"How's Billie?"

"She's fine. Doing fine."

"And you, Evelyn, how's your daughter?"

"Out of law school and clerking."

"Congratulations."

Evelyn smiled. She uncrossed her legs, leaned forward and set down her coffee cup. "I saw your son in the paper. Won't be long before he's running your law firm while you're over here running the city."

Honeycutt poured himself some more coffee. "You know why we're here, Frank. Primary's in June. Last time we spoke about it, you said you hadn't really looked over the candidates yet. Have you had a chance to think about it?"

"Donald, you know I have a lot of respect for you and Billie. You've helped me in all my races, and I don't forget a friend."

"But—" Evelyn said.

The mayor nodded. "I'll be honest with you. Kate Blackthorne is almost family, so it's a hard decision. But it will be either you or her."

"If you're looking for us to sweeten the pot—" Evelyn said.

He held up his hand. "Absolutely not. I know I can count on you to do the right thing by the city. This really is personal for me, which is why it's so hard."

Honeycutt set down his cup and stood up, which made Evelyn and the mayor stand up as well. "I appreciate your candor, Frank. No hard feelings." They shook hands. "Just remember. I'm going to win the primary. I've got the best chance of beating Daniels in the fall. Whoever gets on board early enough to help—well, I'm going to have to look after them first."

"I understand. That goes without saying." He glanced at Evelyn. "Good to see you."

Honeycutt and Evelyn left the mayor's office and got their coats off the coat rack in the outer office. Sharon, the mayor's office coordinator, phone cradled between her ear and her shoulder, gave them a short nod and a smile. Honeycutt smiled back, trying hard not to look angry. Evelyn pushed through the mayor's office door ahead of him, and they started down the subway-tiled hallway to the parking lot.

Honeycutt shrugged his hands into his coat pockets. "Frank's a piece of work. After all we've done for him."

"I'm not surprised," Evelyn said. "That's his standard ploy, all sincerity and understanding."

"So?"

"He's with Blackthorne, but he'll try to avoid endorsing anyone if he can. He'll try to wait until it's clear who's going to win, then he'll pile on."

"He's a coward."

"That's why he's mayor. Being mayor is not about being decisive; it's about balancing all the city's competing interests so that you can get enough votes in the next election. He's a master at that. And when you're in Congress, he'll give you all the support he can without taking any blame."

Honeycutt's phone rang. It was Billie. "Honey, how are you?"

"I'm fine. I've got to take a rain check on lunch. Can't talk now, but I'll see you at dinner."

"Okay. I'll fill you in on Frank this evening."

"Love you."

"Love you."

Honeycutt put his phone back in his pocket. "So we'll have to be patient with Frank."

"He'll have to come around after we line up everyone else."

They pushed through the enamel green double doors into the parking lot. "Need a ride? My car is just across the street at the bank," Honeycutt said.

Evelyn shook her head. "It's only a few blocks."

"You sure? I've got a few minutes."

"I'm fine. The walk will do me good."

Sheriff's deputy Marvin Gruber pulled up into the driveway of 861 Riverview Heights. The garage door was closed, and a 2014 red Lexus was parked in the driveway. Deputy Gruber was skinny, five feet eight, with a brown crew cut, big hands, and a hawk nose. He was thirty years old, married with two toddlers, and hoping for promotion to chief deputy. He was wearing an olive-green sheriff's department uniform and coat. He put on his sheriff's department cap after he got out of his cruiser. Mrs. Wolfe, a slim forty-five-year-old woman wearing department store fashion, opened the door. "Finally," she said. "What took so long?"

"There's been a break-in, ma'am?"

"What do you think?" She pointed to the dining room. There was dry white liquid splattered across the walnut table and brown liquid congealing on the oak floor. He followed her from the two-story entry through the dining room into the kitchen. The kitchen tile floor was an explosion of refrigerator contents: broken sauce jars of various colors splattered across the brick-red tile with lettuce, zucchini, and pear mashed into the mix.

"This is what it looked like when you got home?"

Mrs. Wolfe pushed a strand of blond hair behind her ear. "We were up at our cabin. Just got home this morning. The neighbors who called us told us that the deputies who came that night said not to touch anything until you came to look."

He nodded. "Yes, ma'am. We wanted you here before we went through the house." He looked around. "Anything other than this damage? Anything missing or broken elsewhere in the home?"

She shook her head. "Just damage to the family room sofa and carpet."

"If you notice anything over the next few days, give me a call." He handed her his card.

"This neighborhood used to be safe."

"Yes, ma'am. In the paperwork it says you were broken into last year. Lost some jewelry."

"That's why we got the alarm system."

He nodded. "We're increasing patrols, asking people to be on the lookout for suspicious types."

"Who do you think did it?"

"If I had to guess, looks like stoners. Hate to say it, but it could be neighborhood kids. They get high, start acting out. Next day they're ashamed, except when they're bragging to their friends. You should get your alarm checked out. Looks like they were here a good ten minutes before it kicked over."

"So that's it? No fingerprinting?"

"Not for something like this. Cutbacks. Sorry. Now, if they stole something valuable, something traceable, like guns or jewelry, it might warrant an investigation."

She shook her head.

He nodded. "Well, then, sorry it took so long for me to get here. We'll keep our eyes open. You can go ahead and clean up."

She closed the door behind him, went back into the kitchen, and picked up her cell phone off the counter. "Gary? The deputy just left. They're not going to do anything. I already miss the jewelry. Wish we hadn't reported it stolen last year."

"We didn't have any other choice. We had to have the insurance money to make the balloon payment on the mortgage."

"I still think we should have reported the money and the wine."

"Then we'd have to explain why we've got large amounts of cash in the house. I don't want to end up with the IRS snooping around our wholesale purchases and our retail sales, and the wine just points to a lot of disposable income."

"It's all so frustrating."

"I know. At least your mom's stuff was in the safety deposit box. The rest of it is replaceable."

"That doesn't make it any easier."

"Get Kelly to help you clean up. I'll see you at dinner."

That evening, Honeycutt and Billie sat in the dark on the sofa in their living room, sipping Martinis and enjoying the fire in their white marble fireplace. Their living room was a traditional space, with a huge Persian rug, dark wood wainscoting, and a sofa and matching chairs with carved wooden legs. A drinks cabinet was built into one corner of the room. They were still dressed from their workday. The smell of baked chicken wafted in from the kitchen. Billie sat back and sighed. "I love the crackle of real wood. I'm glad the designer didn't talk me into going with gas."

Honeycutt patted her leg. "So long as I don't have to clean the fireplace, I'm happy."

She sipped her drink. "How was your day?"

"How was your day? You're the one who had to skip lunch."

"I ate with Ricardo at that new Thai place. I'm beginning to think he'd rather sleep with me than buy that property."

"So are you?"

She gave him an appraising look. "When did you start drinking? I've got enough on my hands with you."

He chuckled. "Maybe that property is just going to have to sit for a while."

"I'm tired of taking care of it and there's not enough to do to hire a manager. Besides, I'd rather spend my time on my charity projects."

"That's your strength."

"Thank you." She set her half-finished drink on the end table. "Enough about that. What did Frank have to say?"

"He said it was me or Blackthorne, but it was complicated. Evelyn said he was going with Blackthorne but hedging his bets."

"She's right. That's what he's trying for, but he's screwed. I'm lining up the downtown business association. We're going to put together a campaign war chest, and we're all going to support the same people. So the mayor can jump on board or he can go it alone."

Honeycutt shook his head. "I'd hate to be going up against you."

She picked up her glass and tipped it toward him. "Damn straight." She downed the rest of her drink.

"Want another?"

"No." She sat back again and took his hand in hers. She looked into the crackling fire. "You're going to win the primary. We're going to crush Barney Daniels in the fall. War hero or not, he hasn't done a thing in forever. In January, we'll be renting an apartment in DC. It will be the beginning of our new lives on the coast." She looked into his eyes. "Donny, I love you so much."

"Me too, honey. Me too." He set his drink down, leaned over, and kissed her softly.

3: The Missing Money

Two months later, the snow had melted and the grass was starting to green, even if there was still a frosty chill in the morning air. Out at the Hillside Motel by the old freeway ramp, a red Lincoln and a white Cadillac were parked in front of the black door to a room on the far side of the tan concrete block building. Inside the faded room, Honeycutt and Roslyn stood beside the king-size bed pulling at each other's clothes and kissing. "I missed you," she said.

"Not much time."

They fell on the bed, still locked together, Roslyn on top. "This place is a dump. It's even worse than last place." She kissed him.

"That's why we'll never get caught here." He kissed her. "You know any long-haul truck drivers?"

She studied his face. "Have you found out anything about the blackmailers?"

"Nothing." He shook his head. "Still paying. Everything's quiet." He slipped his hand into her unbuttoned blouse.

"Careful with the clothes." She shifted off of him and got to her feet. "I have to look sharp today."

She padded to the closet in her stocking feet and hung her suit jacket and blouse on hangers. Honeycutt watched her slink out of her suit pants before he rolled off the rust colored bedspread and pulled off his clothes, laying his suit jacket and pants carefully over the back of a chair. After he took off his boxers, he turned and looked at her. She was still wearing a tiny white lace thong and a white lace push-up bra. She turned in a circle so that he could see her front and back, then she smiled and walked slowly over to the bed, where she pulled back the covers and lay down on her stomach in the saddle in the middle of the bed. Honeycutt straddled her, unhooked her bra, and pushed the straps up over her shoulders. "Turn over."

She giggled. "Make me."

Billie sat at her desktop computer in her home office. A cup of coffee sat on her left side; a yellow legal pad and a mechanical pencil sat on her right. She didn't have any appointments until after her yoga class, so she was catching up on the financials and balancing the checkbooks for the last few months. At both the end of January and end of February, $10,000 in cash had been taken out of Donald's checking account, but all of his expenses by check, debit, or credit were the same as usual. There was a knock at the door to her office. She looked over her shoulder. "Yeah?"

Mamie peeked in. "We're cleaning upstairs today."

"Do my bathroom first."

Mamie shut the door. Billie picked up her cell phone. Donald's phone rang eight times before he answered. "Hey, hon, what's up? I'm in a meeting. Can I call you back?"

"What were the ten-thousand-dollar withdrawals for at the end of January and February?"

"Ten thousand? Campaign business. I'll call later."

Billie switched accounts. The campaign account didn't show any $10,000 deposits. Was he already handing out cash under the table? Surely he wasn't paying the interns. She called Evelyn. "Hey, I want to word this very carefully, because I don't want to know what I don't want to know."

"Okay," Evelyn replied.

"Have you been making a lot of payments requiring cash?"

"Long and short answer. No. We've been making no cash payments to speak of. And the few we have, for small sums, I have every receipt. You know how I feel about recordkeeping. Why?"

"Just hit by a blast of paranoia, I guess. Less than three months left to the primary—this is about the time for things to go off the rails. Glad to hear that you have the covers tied down tight."

"That's what you pay me for."

"I'll talk to you later."

Billie set her phone down and took a sip of coffee. It was cold. She turned from the computer screen and looked out the window. The trees were still bare. Donald couldn't be that stupid, could he? He'd promised to lay off the bimbos until after the election. He'd lied about the money, so he must be doing something he didn't want her to know about. Maybe it was something stupid that wasn't women. But that was his only weakness. He'd screw anything in tight clothes that was willing, which seemed to be most of them. What kind of trouble had he gotten himself into? Whatever it was, it had to stop. He was going to be Representative Honeycutt, then Senator Honeycutt. And she was going to be standing beside him calling the shots. Anything that got in the way had to be dealt with. What to do? She didn't want to go to Bo. He was Tommy's brother and he was the sheriff, but he'd never liked Donny. Besides, he might not be able to cover up whatever he found out. No, this was a private investigation. She picked up her phone. Stan Jessup was the person she needed to talk to.

"Good morning, Stan." She pictured him slouched back in his office chair with his feet up on the corner of his desk, a beefy hand holding the phone against his shaved head, his toothbrush mustache bobbing as he spoke into the receiver.

"Ms. Honeycutt, what can I do for you?"

"I've got a delicate job. No one can know."

"Have I ever let you down?"

"I want my husband followed."

The line was silent for a moment.

"Stan?"

"Yes, ma'am. I was just a little surprised. No problem. I'll put a GPS tracker on him."

"I want eyes."

"Human surveillance will cost you, ma'am."

"I don't care. Just make sure he doesn't find out."

"I'll put my best operative on him. What are we looking for?"

Billie swallowed hard. "Adultery."

"Hard evidence? Pictures?"

"Yes. And Stan, maybe I'm wrong. Maybe it's something else. Whatever it is, I want to know."

"Yes, ma'am."

She set down her phone. Spying on Donny. This is what it had come to. When had she quit trusting him? He was a good man, reliable, dependable in every way except when it came to skirt chasing. It hadn't seemed like such a big deal when she married him. They seemed so perfect for each other, so perfect for her plans to go to Washington and take her wheeling and dealing to the next level without having to be in office herself. But now? Adultery was just the kind of problem that could derail the election. But maybe she was overreacting. Maybe he was gambling. It wasn't drugs or drink, that was for sure. God-damn him. She pushed back in her chair. Why couldn't he have come to her? Why couldn't he have told the truth? Well, whatever it was, Stan would ferret it out. She picked up her pencil and tried to refocus on the bank statement on her computer monitor, but she just couldn't concentrate anymore. She felt anxious and empty, as if her future were no longer in her own hands. She needed to move around. She grabbed her coffee cup and went to the kitchen for a refill.

It was 4:00 p.m. when Honeycutt hurried out into the parking lot of the First National Bank and got into his Cadillac. Traffic was busy, as busy as it ever got in Randal Junction for the fifteen minutes when traffic might be stop and go, but the county commission meetings weren't set as a convenience to those who had to drive to them, they were set as a convenience to the employees who had to attend and wanted to eat a late supper with their families. Honeycutt hoped the meeting would be short. According to the agenda, there was nothing out of the ordinary and no new business to cause an uproar. There seldom was in an election year. Farm air quality, water runoff standards, housing eating up farmland—it was all bob and weave until after the elections, when lame ducks would try to make things hard for their enemies while they planned their return in two years. He pulled out onto First Street. He was driving against the traffic, so all he really had to be concerned about were drivers making left turns out of parking lots and side streets. He called Billie and got her voicemail. "Just wanted to remind you I've got county commission, so I won't be home for supper. Hope you had a good day."

He found an empty parking spot in the employee lot behind the county courthouse, got his parking tag out of his glove box and set it on the dash, and then jogged into the limestone building to get out of the sharp March wind. The clouds were churning like there might be rain sometime after dark.

Out on the street, Cindi Butler, Stan Jessup's associate, watched Honeycutt run into the courthouse. She drove her old blue Ford Taurus around the square, looking for a parking spot where she could watch his Cadillac and the courthouse side entrance that would remain unlocked after 5:00 p.m. She found one across the street in front of Ace Printing. She settled in, lowered her window a few inches, and turned off her car. Cindi was a full-figured black woman with shoulder-length relaxed hair, which she believed gave her a very white-friendly look. She zipped up her blue down coat, thought about getting a hot cup of coffee from the PourAway coffee shop on the corner while she knew Honeycutt wasn't going anywhere, but decided against it. She didn't want to need the bathroom later when it might make a difference. She turned on her radio to the news and settled back to watch the side entrance and the Cadillac. She hated surveillance. Her boys would be home from high school, and she wanted to be there to check on homework and make them a nutritious supper. Make sure they weren't up to some after-school foolishness. Oh, well, this didn't come up too often, and Stan was easy enough to work for. Much better pay than the security guard job. Flexible hours. Got to carry a gun to protect herself.

She watched while the other county commissioners arrived. She took a list out of her coat pocket and checked them off. All there. She waited a few more minutes, then she picked up the GPS tracker off the passenger's seat, turned it on, made sure the magnetic case was locked tight, and crossed the street with the tracker in her hand. She stopped next to Honeycutt's car as if she had dropped something and attached the tracker to the steel

frame in one smooth motion. Then she went into the courthouse, used the public restroom to wash her hands, and crossed
back to her car. She got out her company smartphone and
dialed up the GPS tracker. There it was, a blinking red dot on a
map. She set her seat back a few inches and waited.

At 7:15 p.m., Honeycutt, chin down, holding his overcoat
closed with one hand, rushed out of the courthouse, jumped
into his car, and hurried away. Cindi followed him a block
behind, easy work even in the dark, the street lamps reflecting
brightly off of the white Cadillac and the GPS tracker showing
on the smartphone map. They drove twenty minutes down First
Street, past the new strip mall, over the railroad tracks, and
headed in the opposite direction from Honeycutt's house. They
took a right turn onto Elm. Four blocks later, Honeycutt turned
into the Safe Lights Bible Church, a small church in what looked
like it had once been a medium-size big-box store. There were a
dozen cars in the potholed parking lot. Cindi parked in the dark
on the side of the street where she had a good view of the
Cadillac. Honeycutt hurried across the parking lot, coat open,
half-turned just outside the front door, and held out his car key
fob. The lights flashed on the Cadillac, and he disappeared
inside. Cindi wondered how long he was going to be. She called
home on her personal cell phone. Her younger son answered
the phone. "Marcus. How was school?"

"Fine."

"You eat the chili I left on the stove?"

"Uh-huh."

"Homework all done?"

"Most of it."

"What you doing now?"

"Playing a game."

"Pause it, and get your homework done."

"How about I finish the game first?"

"Homework has to be done, all correct, tonight."

"Yes, momma."

"Let me talk to your brother."

"He's not here."

"Where is he?"

"Went to Cicilee's to study."

"He got the cell phone?"

"It's on the kitchen counter."

"What's Cicilee's number?"

"I don't know."

"What's her momma's name?"

"Don't know. Her last name is Grimes, I think."

"See you in a bit. Get your homework done."

Cindi put her cell phone back in her coat pocket. Cicilee. She seemed like a smart girl, but Cindi couldn't remember if there was any adult supervision at her house. She glanced over at the church. He must be in Bible study or something. She picked up the company smartphone, switched screens to Google, and tracked down Cicilee Grimes's phone number.

"Hello, this is Cindi Butler. Could I speak to James, please?"

"Cindi, this is Janice. How are you? They're up to Cicilee's room studying. I'll get him."

Cindi tried to remember what Janice Grimes looked like, but she just couldn't place her, even though her voice sounded familiar. Now Cicilee, Cindi was sure she'd met her — tall and skinny, happy eyes, pretty smile, cornrowed hair. She needed to keep an eye on her.

"Momma?"

Cindi took a deep breath. "James, what are the rules?"

"I was just over here studying for Spanish."

"Rules?"

"Leave the house, call, take the cell."

"And?"

"I just forgot the cell."

"Just forgot to call. Get on home. Now."

"Momma —"

"When I get home your homework better be done."

She switched the smartphone back to the GPS tracker, which was flashing happily. Cindi sat another thirty minutes. The church parking lot was quiet. No one had driven or walked by. The clouds had blown off and the wind had died down. It was 8:30 p.m. Nothing was going to happen tonight. Besides, the GPS tracker would provide a record of wherever he went. She needed to see about her boys. She started her car and headed home.

At 7:30 a.m., Cindi was parked on the street outside the Honeycutts' house, a two-story white-painted brick with a three-car garage in an older, established neighborhood near the downtown, where all the houses sat on large lots with huge, old trees and deep front yards. A row of low bushes that ran along the brick sidewalk next to the driveway was just starting to fill out with tiny yellow flowers, and the lawn had the deep green color that only came from fertilizer. Cindi glanced down at the smartphone she had laid on the passenger's seat. It showed the map with the flashing dot that indicated that Honeycutt's Cadillac was still at home. When she'd left her house at 7:00 a.m., Marcus and James were up and dressed. They would easily make it to the bus stop in time. She wouldn't have to give them another thought until after cross-country practice ended at 5:00 p.m. She sipped some coffee from her travel cup. A group of middle-school-age students, boys and girls, walked by on the sidewalk, chattering away amiably. Cindi didn't like surveillance hours, but she did like the overtime. Maybe they could afford a vacation this summer if they didn't go too far away. At the end of the summer, but before the start of football practice, so the boys could max out their summer jobs. The smartphone buzzed. It was Stan. She took the call.

"Good morning, Cindi. Where you at?"

"On the street in front of the subject's."

"Where did he go last night?"

"Courthouse at four p.m., Safe Lights Bible Church at seven forty, and according to the GPS, he went home at nine twenty-three."

"You left him at the church?"

"Yeah."

"How do you know he didn't leave in another car and come back?"

"How do I know he didn't bang the church secretary in a closet? Jesus, Stan, he was in the building at eight thirty. He didn't have time to go anywhere."

"I get paid to do a job. I pay you to do a job. We do the job."

"Okay, okay. It won't happen again."

"Thank you. You're a good worker, Cindi; I just can't have any mistakes on this job. Billie Honeycutt is an important client."

She rolled her eyes. Sometimes Stan was a pain in the ass. She didn't want to listen to him anymore. "Subject's backing down the driveway."

"Good luck." He hung up.

Cindi put the smartphone back onto the map with the flashing red dot. She took a sip of coffee and kept focused on the Honeycutts' garage doors. She needed to stay alert. Honeycutt would probably be leaving any time now.

Later that morning, Billie sat on the sofa at the far end of the mayor's office. She wore a black pantsuit with a white, scooped-neck shirt and a single strand of pearls. She hadn't touched her coffee. Her red-brown hair was pulled back into a tight bun. She was striving for a severe, take-no-prisoners, come-to-Jesus look. The mayor sat across from her, looking fat, old, and tired, as if he weren't used to taking 9:00 a.m. meetings. His gray suit was already rumpled and his coffee cup was already empty. His mouth was formed up in his half-apology smile.

"That won't be any problem." He moved his hand toward the coffee pot as if he might pick it up, but he didn't. "We're always happy to help the Downtown Business Association with the spring street fair. Blocking off access to the courthouse square, rerouting traffic, Porta Potties—all the usuals. Have you chosen this year's theme?"

"There's a committee—Do you know Robert Hodges? Belinda's husband?"

He nodded.

"He's leading that up. I imagine we'll all know in the next few weeks."

"Great."

"Yeah, it's wonderful to have a big show of unity before the election season really gets underway and anybody's feelings get hurt."

"How's that?"

"The Downtown Business Association is going to be bundling this year to maximize our clout. Fred, Sheila, Marcus,

31

everyone. It's never been done before, so we're hoping for a big impact."

"The DBA backing Donald?"

"Of course, Frank, otherwise we wouldn't be bundling." She stood up and the mayor stood up with her. "I know the primary doesn't matter to you. Who knows? Maybe no one will run against you in the fall. But if you want our support, you need to come out for Donald. Tit for Tat."

"You're putting me in a hard place, Billie."

"I know how it is, Frank. Your favorite aunt's son goes out using your name without permission to land a job out of his league. It's the price we all pay for being in politics where we grew up. You can't help it if your cousin's working for Blackthorne, and I can't help it. If it were your son, I'd give you a pass, but we both know your son is too smart to make a bone-head play like that."

"You're going to owe me some consideration."

"Of course."

"I'll be expecting help with the federal block grant."

She nodded.

"And some legal work thrown toward my law firm."

"No problem." She stuck out her hand. The mayor shook it.

"I'm glad we're on the same team, Frank. I really would have felt bad about jamming you up."

"When do you want the announcement?"

"Hold off. We want all of our endorsements to flood out together in one big ad campaign."

"Whatever you say."

"Give my best to your wife. And tell your cousin no hard feelings. I mean it."

Billie put on her coat in the outer office and then walked down the hall to the parking lot. She took out her phone. "Donald? Frank's on board."

"That was quick."

"He doesn't want to be left out in the cold."

"Can we trust him?"

"He'd double-cross his mother. The one thing we can count on is that he'll always turn to stay in the light."

Cindi sat in her Taurus in the on-street parking across from the First National Bank. Half of a corned beef sandwich wrapped in deli paper was in the seat beside her. An empty chip bag lay on the floor at her feet. A cup of Diet Coke with a straw in it sat in the cup holder. Her eyes were trying to close. Times like these made her wish she still smoked. She scooted into a more up-right position and turned on the radio. Music wouldn't do the trick. She needed to find some talk radio she could just barely tolerate. Nothing like anger to keep a person awake. She cycled through the dial. No luck. Her reception at this spot was horrible. Maybe if she inched forward a few feet. She saw movement in her peripheral vision. Honeycutt was crossing the bank's parking lot. He got into his car and pulled out. Cindi started her car and followed him. He drove out of the down-town and took First Street going north until Simmons Boulevard, where he turned right. The traffic was light. Cindi lay back a block, following him via the smartphone. In the northeast part of town, he turned into Maplewood Estates, a mature neighborhood of two-car garage houses that were built after Maplewood Elementary School was built in 1972.

Honeycutt parked on the street in front of a split-level house with tan brick and tan vinyl siding. The lawn was freshly cut. A real estate agent's FOR SALE sign was prominently displayed in the middle of the yard. A woman wearing a gray pantsuit, with a teal scarf around her neck—probably a real estate agent—stood outside a red Lincoln parked in the driveway. Cindi drove past and turned around at the end of the block. She pulled over and parked on the street. Honeycutt and the woman shook hands as if they were just meeting, but there was something about their interaction that seemed rehearsed. They went into the house. Cindi sat watching the front of the house for a few minutes, when it suddenly occurred to her that the woman bore a striking resemblance to Billie Honeycutt. Same brown-red hair, same general build. It wasn't her, but she could pass for her in the distance.

Cindi reached into the backseat for her camera and double-checked the power level. The camera was completely charged and ready to go. She crossed the street, walked up the driveway past the Lincoln, and looked into the living room. The house appeared to be fully furnished. She could see light-colored oak furniture and a green-and-white checked sofa paired with a green recliner. She glanced up and down the street. No one was outside. She couldn't hear any cars. She ducked behind the bank of evergreen bushes on the split-level side of the entryway and crouched down to peek into the lower window. Light fell into the room from the hallway. A little girl's bedroom: white-framed unicorn poster on the wall, pink-trimmed bed, and a row of ballerina dolls on the top bookshelf.

Cindi continued around the side of the house. The backyard was fenced with a four-foot-high chain-link fence. There was no gate on this side. Cindi looked down at her mud-splattered shoes. They were flats, but they weren't meant for fence climbing. She sighed, slung the camera over her shoulder, and started climbing up the fence. Just as she reached the top, she noticed the doghouse in the far left corner of the backyard. Where was the dog? She whistled. No barking. No running. She whistled again. Then she threw her leg over and hopped down into the yard. The lower window was dark, but the upper window was lit up.

A paint-splattered aluminum ladder lay on its side against the back of the house. Cindi picked it up and leaned it gently against the side of the house to the right of the upper window. She stepped up on the first rung. The left rail of the ladder sank three or four inches into the earth. She tugged down on the other rail, got it to sink about two inches, and very gingerly climbed up to peek into the window, trying all the while to keep her weight to the right on the ladder rungs. The left rail sunk a few more inches, putting the ladder at an angle on the wall. She gripped the windowsill to keep the ladder from shifting onto the glass. She looked in the window. She could see to the right. It was a boy's room. Football posters hung on one wall. A TV with a game console sat against the wall at the end of the bed. She shifted her body on the ladder so she could lean her head over to see straight in. On the bed, Honeycutt and the woman were tangled together. Cindi smiled. Time to earn her pay. She hooked her arm through the ladder so she could use both hands and turned off the camera's flash. The ladder teetered. She grabbed the windowsill with her right hand, stuck the camera out in front of the window with her left hand, and shot six pictures as fast as she could. Then she looked at the screen on the back of the camera to see if she had some keepers. Four definite ones. Time to get down.

She eased back down the ladder, keeping her weight to the right. Now the left side had sunk about five inches into the ground. She glanced down at her shoes. The toes were marked from where she climbed the fence, but the shoes weren't ruined yet. She gripped the ladder, held it out from the wall, and stepped back and forth to loosen it from the ground. Then she pulled up and repeated the process until she got the ladder free. She carried it to the chain-link fence, leaned it against the rail, climbed the ladder to get to the top the fence, hopped over, and then tipped the ladder backward into the yard. It rattled like distant thunder when it bounced off the ground. She stood against the wall of the house, listening, but everything was quiet. No time to waste.

Back around the front, she took a picture of the red Lincoln and its license plate, the front of the house showing the address, and the Lincoln and Honeycutt's Cadillac. Then she got back into her Taurus. When they came out, she took their picture as they came down the front walk acting very professional. Then she lay back in her seat while Honeycutt drove away. She let him go. She could track him via GPS. She was more interested in where the red Lincoln was going.

She followed the Lincoln out of Maplewood Estates and back down Simmons Boulevard west toward First Street. But instead of turning onto First, the Lincoln continued through the light and turned into Simmons Lanes strip mall. Simmons Lanes Bowling Alley anchored the mall. A coffee shop, a sports bar, Goodwill, and Murray Real Estate strung out down the parking lot beside it. The red Lincoln parked in a spot near the real estate offices. The woman got out and went inside. Cindi parked where she could watch the Lincoln and the front of the real estate offices. She picked up the half of the corned beef sandwich left from her lunch, took a bite, and chased it with a slurp of watered-down Diet Coke. She rewrapped the sandwich and put it back in the passenger's seat. She wasn't really hungry. Twenty minutes passed. Her eyelids felt heavy. She yawned. It was midafternoon, and the adrenalin from getting the pictures had flushed through her system, but she needed to focus on her target and stay awake. She couldn't risk a run to the coffee shop, couldn't take the chance that the woman might leave in the meantime. Every place this woman went provided valuable information about who she was. Cindi propped her elbow against her car door and leaned her head on her hand.

Thirty minutes later, the woman came back out and got into her car. Cindi followed her east on Simmons. She turned into one of the new apartment complexes that had been built next to the new golf course. Cindi followed her down the winding street, trying to stay as far back as she could without losing her. The woman parked in front of a one-story brick apartment on the end of a row near a park-like open area with trees and picnic tables. Cindi pulled into the nearby visitor parking. The woman got out with her briefcase in one hand and her coat slung over her other arm. She went into the apartment. Cindi wrote down the number. Then she called Stan. "Hey, I've got the whole package. Just tailed the woman home. Do you want me to get back on Mr. Honeycutt or do you want to meet?"

"I'll meet you at the office in thirty minutes."

Cindi parked in her usual spot at the end of the back parking lot at Overmeyer Professional Office Building, a row of one-story concrete and red brick offices. The sun had just slipped out from behind the clouds, creating a sudden brightness that reminded her that spring was on the way, even though the air was crisp, and the pavement still had winter damp in the shade. She pushed through the glass door marked "JESSUP INVESTIGATIONS." The outer office, three orange cubicles, a worn, brown leather sofa and a magazine rack filled with out-of-date magazines, was empty. Through the door to the conference room, she could see Jessup seated at the long, wood-grain-topped table amid stacks of open file folders and loose papers. "Whoa," he yelled, "there she is: the man of the hour, bringing home the bacon. Get on back here."

Cindi couldn't help smiling. Stan was fifty-two years old, shaved-head bald, with a gray-brown mustache and a military bearing. He always wore a tan sports coat with leather patches on the elbows, new jeans, and snakeskin cowboy boots. When she described him to her boys, she said he was so white-man-square that he was almost hip. "Sit down, sit down," he said, "and fill me in."

"They were shacking up at a for-sale house. Walked in the front just like they were touring property."

"Give me the camera."

She passed the camera across to him. "It's all set up."

He looked at the screen on the back of the camera. Honeycutt and Roslyn were groping on a single bed that was covered with a Star Wars comforter. "Hot damn."

Cindi nodded. "They are some healthy folks."

He looked up. "She looks sort of like —"

"Yeah, that's what tipped me off. Got pics of her car, them coming out together. Tailed her to Murray Real Estate and then home."

"Very nice work. But, then, you were trained by the best."

"If you say so."

He sat back, flipping through the pictures.

She smiled. "So, am I done?"

He clicked his teeth. "Let's not get in a hurry. Billables are light this month. We shouldn't call it off until Ms. Honeycutt says so. Maybe there's more than one. Maybe she knows about this one already. The money's nothing to her, so let's take it one step at a time."

"I can't keep leaving my boys at home alone."

"Hey, I know the overtime is a two-edged sword. You got your sons up to high school and you can't afford to drop the ball. I understand that. But you're my best operative."

"I've heard it before, Stan."

"Johnny's been with me longer than you, but you think I'm going to trust him with something this sensitive? I can't lay back on what I'm working on. So that just leaves you. I'm not going to forget you stepped up. We get finished with Honeycutt, and there'll definitely be a bonus."

"Definitely?"

"Definitely." He pointed his finger at her. "One day soon your boys will be men, and you'll have the time to make partner. Then you'll be happy you invested in the firm." He set the camera down on a pile of file folders. "Get a new camera from the closet and keep after Honeycutt."

Cindi dialed her phone as she walked across the parking lot to her car. "Ruby? This is Cindi. Could you do me a big favor? I've got to work late again, and I was wondering if you could make sure my boys got a decent meal? Thank you so much. I really appreciate it."

4: The Confession

"Don't try to deny it." Billie stood with her back to the closed door of her home office, her arms crossed and a deep frown on her face. Honeycutt stood beside her antique desk, trying to look innocent without smiling. The sun was low, casting its thin light straight through the wide-slat blinds. They could hear random noises from the kitchen, where Mamie was finishing off the supper that the new girl had made.

Honeycutt, his tie loose around his neck, pushed a file folder out of the way and sat back on the edge of the desk. "I don't know what you've heard."

"Heard?" Billie sat down on the loveseat that was positioned against the wall by the door. She shook her head. "My God, you are so full of shit." She pulled off her high heels and threw one against the wall. From her seat, she had to squint against the light to see him clearly. Her voice rose. "How about seen? Look in that mailer." She pointed with her other shoe.

Honeycutt picked up the mailer with the Jessup Securities address on it. He expected to see the picture of him and Roslyn that the blackmailers had taken; instead he was looking at pictures from yesterday's rendezvous. "You've been spying on me."

Billie sprang up off the loveseat and smacked him across the face. He dropped the pictures and held his arms up in front of his face. "Billie, stop. Stop it. Come on. Enough."

She threw the other shoe down, kicked it, and stood there with tears running down her cheeks. He tried to put his arms around her, but she pushed him away. "How could you lie to me? Now? With the primary coming up? You're supposed to be a Christian. I guess that Bible study didn't take."

He looked at her stockinged feet and kept quiet.

"At least tell me you were wearing a condom." She grabbed some tissues from the box on her desk, blew her nose, and dabbed at her face. "Who is she?"

Honeycutt kept looking at her feet. "Roslyn Harrison. She's a real estate agent. Met her scouting for campaign space."

"She married?"

He looked up. "Yeah. She's married. That's why I thought she was safe." He tried to find Billie's eyes. "Billie, I never meant to hurt you. I'll break it off."

"I know you will."

"I'll never see her again."

"Call her now. Right now."

"Billie—"

"Right now. And I'm going to listen."

He picked up the landline on the desk and called Roslyn's number. Billie stood with her ear next to the other side of the receiver. "Roslyn?" Honeycutt said.

"Hey, you, I was just thinking of you."

"We have to talk."

"Hold on. Traffic is fierce. Let me pull in somewhere." The phone was quiet for a minute. "Okay. What's up?"

"I can't see you anymore."

"What?"

"We were followed yesterday. Billie knows. It's over."

Roslyn started crying into the phone. "No. Listen. We can lay low."

"It's over."

"I can't live without you."

Honeycutt hung up the phone. "See? I know where my loyalties lie."

Billie stepped back away from him. "You put everything we worked for at risk."

"I'm sorry. I'll make it up to you. I'll win this election for you."

"We had an agreement. Now I had to have you watched. Do you know how humiliating that is?"

"What else can I say? You knew what I was like when you married me."

"Yeah," she nodded, "and I don't care if you're screwing around when it doesn't matter. But now it matters. We agreed. Besides, I do care that other people know that I let you, even if I'm paying them."

"She's married. She has as much to lose as me. That's why there wasn't any risk."

"No means no. That was the agreement until after the election. You think you can sneak around on me? I'll always find out. There's always a money trail."

"Money trail?"

"Don't play innocent. You've been taking cash from the accounts to spend on your new best friend."

"Billie, I didn't spend that money on her."

Her mouth fell open. "Then what—"

"You better sit down."

"I'm not sitting down." She poked her finger into his chest. "You're going to tell me the truth. Right now. How many girls are there?"

Honeycutt held his hands up, surrender style. "She was the only one. I swear to God. I was being as careful as I've ever been, sweetie, but back in January I got an envelope with pictures and a DVD of me and Roslyn."

"In bed?"

He nodded.

"Sweet Jesus."

"I've been paying until I could figure out what to do."

"In the middle of the primary season."

"On the bright side, it's not politics, or it would already be out."

"Bright side? Sometimes, I don't know why I love you. You'd test the patience of Jesus Christ. Until this is dealt with and hushed up, it could come out at any time. Tomorrow, next week, the week before the primary. Hell, you think Daniels won't dig? They'd let us spend our money and then put the pictures in the media when it's too late for us to mount a denial, just to seal the deal. That's what I'd do. After the election's lost, no one will care about the how or why.

"I know. I'm not an idiot. I just didn't know what to do."

"You mean you just didn't know what to do to fix the blackmail and to keep me from finding out about the bimbo."

He sat on the sofa and rested his head in his hands. "Fair enough. I've fucked this all up. I've racked my brain, I've been over and over it, but I still don't know how to fix this."

Billie stood in front of him and touched his shoulder. "That's why you should have come to me to begin with. Promise me you won't make that mistake again."

He looked up at her. "I know. I know. I should have sucked it up and told you. So what are we going to do?"

She walked to the window and looked out through the blinds. The sun was still shining. The plants were growing. The birds and chipmunks were happily foraging. Everything was as it should be. She turned. "I'm going to go see Bo after dinner. I bet he'll have some ideas."

"I don't think he'll help me."

She snorted. "Bo? You'll never measure up to Tommy, far as he's concerned. He'd never help you. But he'd do anything for me."

"I'm sorry I lied. Bils, I'm so sorry."

She looked at the mailer on her desk. "Don't even think you can sweet talk your way out of this. This is not that kind of hurt."

It was nearly eight p.m. by the time Billie walked into the sheriff's office at the county jail. Bo Teardale was sitting behind his gray metal desk, reading a report on his laptop. He hadn't played football in college, but he looked like he had. He was a big man, with strong arms and shoulders, a large, round head covered in thinning blond hair combed straight back, and a beer belly that didn't look like it would slow him down in a fight. He wore the sheriff's department uniform: tan long-sleeve shirt, olive pants, and black boots. His gun belt hung on the corner of his desk. "Hey, Billie," he said. He laid his black frame glasses on the desk and motioned to one of the two oak armchairs facing his desk.

"Bo." Billie sat down in her coat and smiled wearily.

The sheriff reached down into a desk drawer and brought out two coffee cups, followed by a bottle of bourbon. He held the bottle up toward her. She nodded. He poured two drinks and put the bottle back in the drawer. "You look like you been rode hard and put away wet, girl. What's on your mind?"

Billie picked up her cup, took a sip, and held it in both hands. "Sometimes, Bo, I'm surprised by how much you and Tommy look alike."

He shrugged. "You can blame our dad."

"You still like being sheriff?"

"Think I'll stay as long as the people let me."

"Even though Sally left you?"

"Yeah, well, that was hard. But I don't think she left me for being sheriff. I think she left me for being me."

"And you've got your son and your daughter to be proud of."

He nodded. "You're beginning to sound a little morbid. Everything all right at home?"

She took another sip from her cup. "No, I can't say it is."

"How can I help?"

Billie told him about Donald's infidelity and the blackmail. "Can you stop it? Keep it hushed up?"

The sheriff looked at the right wall of his office, which was covered in pictures of family vacations and fishing trips. Up in the right hand corner was a picture of him with Tommy and Sally and Billie when they were camping out at the reservoir before he was sheriff. "You could run someone else. You could run yourself. You'd win easier than Donald."

She shook her head. "I don't want to be a congressman. I want to be a congressman's wife."

"All the power and none of the headache?"

"You know me. Besides, Evelyn will do better managing Donald."

"When you first started putting your hopes on him, I told you that you were shooing your ducks to a shallow pond."

"I still love him, Bo. I know it's crazy, but I still think he might turn out to be something."

"Well, then. Your mind's made up. I can't promise anything, but I'll do my best."

"Thank, Bo. I don't know what I'd do without you."

"That's enough of that talk. We'll get this straightened out."

Billie finished her drink, set her cup on the edge of the desk, and stood up. The sheriff came around his desk and captured her in a bear hug. "You quit your worrying, girl." He patted her back. "I'll have this problem sorted out before you know it."

George came in the door to their apartment carrying two sacks of groceries. Roslyn, dressed in gray sweat pants and a button-up pajama top with candy canes on it, was standing at the peninsula that divided the kitchen from the rest of the room, reading the latest issue of *Guns and Ammo*. "Where you been?" she asked. "You haven't answered your phone all evening."

"I was stuck showing houses to two night owls without kids. Whenever I thought we were done, they were asking if they could see one more. I forgot about your call." He set the grocery bags on the counter. "Sorry. I have got some cereal and milk, though."

He turned back to the door to hang up his coat. She put a half-gallon of milk and a quart of strawberries into the refrigerator and a large box of Shredded Wheat into the cabinet. "No yogurt?"

"Couldn't remember the brand you were eating."

He came back to the counter and sat on a stool on the living room side. "I'm bushed. Keeping up a cover is the hardest part of this life."

"You want a drink?"

"Fill it to the rim."

She poured two fingers of gin into two glasses, added ice, and slid one across to him.

He looked at her expectantly.

"Get a drink first; then I'll tell you the news."

Icy cold juniper washed down his throat. "Okay, I'm steeled. Let's hear it."

"Donald broke up with me." She went over the phone conversation word for word.

"Sounds ominous enough. His wife could have caught him; she could have been listening while he was talking to you. Or it could all be an excuse. The guy's a serial philanderer. Could be

44

he hates good-byes, and he's got some fresh pussy he's trying to work into the mix."

"You're not helping my ego."

"He's got no taste." George took another drink. "You were crying?"

"I was shocked. Despondent. When I told him I couldn't live without him, I almost believed it myself."

"Well, the next few days will tell."

"You want something to eat?"

"Got some drive-through."

Roslyn got out a jar of peanut butter and a spoon.

"Thought you didn't like peanut butter."

"I don't know. It's just been a long time. Felt like trying it again." She scooped up a spoon of peanut butter and licked it like a lollypop. "Not bad." She looked at the label on the jar. "Maybe it's the brand."

"Anyhow," George continued, "he's still making payments; so we're good there. If he's done with you, it's not all bad. If his wife doesn't know, I can get a payment out of him as the aggrieved husband. If she does know, I'll get her to pay to avoid the publicity. And if neither of those works, I still don't have to share you anymore. It's almost a win-win."

Roslyn set the empty spoon on the counter. "You sure know how to make a girl feel special."

George smiled. "You don't have to sell me to get me in the sack."

"Is that right?"

"All you got to do is lead the way."

Billie stood in her bra and panties in her walk-in closet, hanging up her suit. She looked in the full-length mirror. The fluorescent lights made her look washed out and old. She turned to one side, pulled in her gut, and tightened her quads. Her figure was still excellent. She needed to make an appointment to get her hair touched up and trimmed.

"There you are." She turned around. Honeycutt was standing in the doorway, still dressed in the gray suit and red striped tie he'd put on that morning.

"Where you been?"

"Bible study."

"Oh, yeah. It's Tuesday." She slipped out of her underwear, dropped them into the clothes hamper, and pulled a blue silk sleep shirt on over her head. Honeycutt took a step toward her. She stepped back toward the wall. "Why are you here?"

"Come on, Bils, you know you're the only one I love. I feel so bad."

"Because you got caught?"

"Because you feel bad. You never cared before."

"You lied to me."

"How long are you going to make me pay?"

"I'm going to see a blood test before you get back in my bed."

"Really? You think I've got an STD?" He stepped back toward the door. "Fine. I'll get it taken care of tomorrow. Okay? I promise. Just let me back in."

"Guest room."

"Bils —"

"My heart still hurts."

He stomped out and slammed the bedroom door. She could hear him clomping down the stairs. Probably headed for the whiskey in the drinks cabinet. She turned on her bedside lamp, locked the bedroom door, and turned off the overhead light before she climbed into bed. She lay on her back and stared at the ceiling. She knew she was going to have to get over his betrayal if she were going to make her dreams come true. She just had to find a way to give these feelings up, let them go, and move on. How? Why did Tommy have to die? He'd be the one running for office. It had always been his dream. Representative Teardale. Senator Teardale. He'd have been an easy sell, a sure thing. And he'd never done anything to hurt her. Sure, he could be tactless and tough, but he was always loyal, and he never hurt her on purpose.

She rolled onto her side and pushed the extra pillow up between her legs. She remembered being at the plane crash site: the smell of gasoline, the burning weeds, the sounds of the fire trucks and ambulances, Bo trying to hold her back, her breaking free, Tommy still strapped to a broken seat, his head turned too far around and both his legs broken up at a tight angle. She gripped her head pillow with both her arms and began to sob.

Why Tommy? Why the love of her life? Why did she have to move forward with the second best? Why couldn't it have been Donald in the plane? She gasped. She reached for the tissue box on the night table beside her bed. Is that what it had come to? She had to think about Donald dead to feel better about what he'd done? She'd looked for the most eligible bachelor after she'd finished mourning. Donald was the best man who was available. She'd made her choice. Now she had to find a way to make it work.

5: The Back-up Play

The next morning, Sheriff Teardale drove from the jail across the courthouse square and down Railroad Street to the First National Bank and parked in the bank president's parking space. Sandra Jenkins, the bank president, wouldn't arrive at the bank before 10:00 a.m., and the sheriff would be long gone by then. He'd set this early morning meeting with Honeycutt so that as few bank employees would see him as possible. The morning was cold for late March, and the sky was overcast. Rain was forecast for the afternoon. When he came up to the front door and knocked on the glass, Gladys, the early morning drive-through cashier, looked up from behind the counter and buzzed him in. Honeycutt met him in the lobby. "Bo, glad you could make it. Coffee?"

"Thanks, but I've already had mine."

"Come on back."

Honeycutt led the way to his private office behind a row of unoccupied cubicles. A picture of Billie in a short, strapless summer dress sat on the corner of his otherwise cleared desktop. A big computer monitor sat on a small table perpendicular to the desk. On the wall behind the desk was a large, framed, black-and-white photograph of a lighthouse lighting a rough sea from a rocky point. Honeycutt sat down in the high-backed leather chair behind his desk and gestured toward one of the two low-backed leather chairs facing it. The sheriff sat down and put his cap in the other chair. He gave Honeycutt a disappointed look. "I understand you've got a blackmail problem."

Honeycutt looked at Billie's picture. "I don't know quite how to begin."

"I don't want to know about how you're ruining your marriage. I just want to know about the money."

"I take ten thousand dollars in cash to a PO box at Security Shipping the first of every month."

"Ten thousand dollars? That's it? How long?"

"Since the first of February."

"So you've made two payments."

He nodded.

"And you've got no idea who's doing this?"

He shook his head.

"What about the girl — what's her name?"

"Roslyn? She broke down when I told her. Guess she's afraid of her husband."

"Really?" The sheriff put his cap back on and stood up. "What's the PO box number?"

"Two-eighty-seven."

"Do what you normally do — except for whoring around. I'll see if I can't get to the bottom of this."

Honeycutt stood up. "I really appreciate this, Bo." He came around his desk and stuck out his hand. The sheriff ignored it.

"Don't thank me. Thank God that your wife still loves you."

The sheriff walked back out to his departmental cruiser. Security Shipping. Cody Yu owned that place. Was he the one on the community betterment board? No, that was his dad. Cody was the one whose son had gone wild. Caught him with a group of boys smoking pot out in Janesville Cemetery — when was that? Two, three years ago. Turned him loose and let Cody deal with it. Never had any more trouble from that boy. Cody and his dad were always good for a little help around election time. The sheriff nodded approvingly. This was a man he could work with.

Security Shipping was located on the corner of First and Simmons. Painters were refreshing the yellow stripes between the parking spaces next to the sidewalk in front of the door, so the sheriff pulled into the farthest away handicap spot. He could see Cody through the front windows, waving his arms around while he explained something to the young man who was working the counter this morning. Cody was a small, thin Asian man whose iron-gray hair was cut close on the sides. He wore a green fleece zip-up over running shoes, jeans and a blue-stripe oxford shirt. When the front door opened, he looked over his shoulder. "Sheriff."

"How you doing, Cody?"

"I'm good, I'm good. How about you?"

"Nobody's running against me in the primary, so I feel great."

Cody put a hand on the sheriff's arm and walked him away from the counter toward the wall of mailboxes. "Looking for a political donation?"

The sheriff shook his head. "This is official business. You got a blackmailer renting one of your boxes."

"Really?"

"Yeah. I want to know who's renting box number 287."

"I think, technically, Sheriff, you're supposed to have a search warrant, but if you're sure it's serious."

"I'd appreciate your help."

"Okay, then." He went over to the counter. "Excuse me, Kenny." The young man behind the counter, jeans, buzz cut, blue golf shirt with the logo "SECURITY SHIPPING" on the right chest, stepped out of the way. Cody logged on to the computer. "Earnest Anderson. 321 Calloway Dr."

"Three-twenty-one Calloway? Can you pull up a city map?"

Cody nodded, went to the bookmarks on his computer, and pulled up the map.

"Is there a three hundred block of Calloway?"

"Well," Cody squinted at the map, "no, there isn't."

"Goddamn it, Cody. I bet that guy isn't named Earnest Anderson, either."

"Calm down, Sheriff. People rent a PO box to protect their privacy. There's no crime in that."

"Did you rent the box? Do you know what Mr. Anderson looks like?"

Cody turned to Kenny. "Have you ever seen who gets mail from box 287?"

Kenny shrugged. "I've only seen him once or twice I guess. Just a regular looking guy. Dark hair with gray in it. Average looking. Nothing about him stood out."

The sheriff frowned. He took Cody by the arm and walked him away from the counter. "When he comes in here, I want you to give me a call."

"Shouldn't the city police be dealing with this? I mean, I'm right smack in the middle of town. I don't want to get caught up in a jurisdictional tug of war."

"I hear you. I'm just trying to keep this whole thing quiet. You don't want publicity, the city subpoenaing all your records, making you look like a racketeer. Remember what happened when that rumor got started that your folks were hiring illegals at their restaurant. It was bullshit, but it still hurt them a long time."

"Okay, Sheriff. I understand what you're saying. I just don't want a misunderstanding with the city."

"I'm not planning on making an arrest here in town. I just need to get my hands on this Anderson guy. So let me know when he shows up, and I'll keep you out of it."

"Fair enough."

They shook hands. "Appreciate your help, Cody."

The sheriff drove back downtown. When he turned onto the courthouse square, he noticed Billie's silver Audi parked in front of the PourAway coffee shop. After he parked his cruiser behind the county jail, he walked back across the square. Crows were cawing from high in the oaks on the courthouse lawn, the grass was starting to turn from brown to green, and even though the sky was still overcast, the air did seem to be warming up. As he got closer to the coffee shop, he could see Billie sitting at a table in the front window, sipping on a latte and looking over some papers in a file folder. She glanced up when she heard the bell on the front door, noticed it was him, and waved. He pulled out the chair across from her and sat down. "Glad I caught you."

"Would you like some coffee?"

"No, thanks. I need to keep moving. The day's getting away from me. I have got some news for you." He explained what he'd found out. "So the PO box is just a money drop, and the mystery man probably won't be back until after Donald leaves the next envelope, which means catching him next week after April first."

"You think whoever comes to the PO box is our guy?"

"Don't worry, Billie, either he's the guy or he'll take me to him. One way or another, it's all going to unravel as soon as I get my hands on the PO box guy."

"So that's when we're at risk for publicity."

"Blackmailers don't want publicity, Billie. The threat of prison will send them on their way. Unless you changed your mind and want them arrested."

She shook her head. "I'm just wanting peace of mind."

"All right, then."

She reached across the table and patted his hand. "Thank you, Bo."

"Don't you worry about this anymore. Just keep Donald on a tight leash when he's outside the yard."

At noon, George sat in his gold Avalon in the curbside parking across the street from the First National Bank, waiting for Honeycutt to come out. People were starting to wear their lighter springtime clothes, even though the streets and side-walks were still gritty from the winter buildup of sand, dust and engine exhaust. George watched the pedestrians in the crosswalk half a block ahead of him. His eyes followed a young, blond woman, a teenager, really, in a bright red frock that could barely count as street clothes. She must have been cold. He got a mint out of his pocket and popped it into his mouth. Honeycutt had told Roslyn that his wife had found out about the affair and that's why he had to break it off, but was that the real reason? Or was he just bored with Roslyn and ready to move on? Did he have another woman waiting in the wings? Or was he suspicious of Roslyn's intentions? George wanted to be sure of the situation so that he could exploit it to the fullest extent possible.

At 12:30, Honeycutt hurried out of the bank's side door and got into his Cadillac. George got ready to pull into traffic, but a city bus pulled up to the bus stop just ahead of him and blocked him in. He smacked his hands against the steering wheel. He couldn't see a thing except for people climbing off the bus and getting on. When the bus finally closed its doors and pulled away, Honeycutt was almost out of sight. George sped through the first traffic light while it was orange and moved aggressively through the lunchtime traffic to get into the same traffic light sequence as Honeycutt, when he noticed a blue Taurus that seemed to stay exactly three car lengths behind Honeycutt. An opportunity would come to change lanes or move up, but the Taurus never took it. Was the Taurus shadowing Honeycutt? George pulled back so that he was following the Taurus. Up ahead, across Omega Drive, George saw Honeycutt pull into the gravel parking lot of Vindaloo Palace Indian restaurant. The blue Taurus turned onto Omega Drive, turned around in the first driveway and parked on the street where it could watch Honeycutt's car.

George parked in the restaurant parking, went inside, and ordered takeout at the front counter. He could see Honeycutt seated with two men and a woman, all in suits, looking at menus. After he got his order, he circled around the block and parked on the street half a block behind the Taurus. An hour later, the Taurus pulled out. He followed the Taurus back downtown. They drove by the bank, where Honeycutt parked and went inside. The driver of the Taurus, a black woman, pulled into the parking lot of the KFC on the corner. George pulled into the Pay-N-Pump across the street, where he could watch her from behind the activity at the gas pumps. She made a phone call, and then drove off back toward the bank. George followed her, expecting her to find a parking spot, but she kept on driving up First Street. She turned left on Simmons Boulevard, drove past the Simmons Lanes strip mall, and turned left into the parking for the Overmeyer Professional Office Building.

George crawled down the parking lot as if he were looking for a particular business and watched her climb out of her old car. She was a big girl, dressed like an office worker, her calf-length raincoat flapping behind her as she walked. She pushed through the door marked "JESSUP INVESTIGATIONS." George drove by the door, couldn't see anything through the glass, and then circled around the parking lot and back onto Simmons

Boulevard. Someone was having Honeycutt tailed. It had to be Honeycutt's wife — either that or some political competition. The wife was more likely. So Honeycutt had told Roslyn the truth, and playing the aggrieved husband to try to blackmail Honeycutt on the threat of telling his wife wasn't going to work. The smarter move now was blackmailing the wife on the threat on ruining Honeycutt's political career and making her the laughingstock of the county. The traffic light at the corner with First turned red. George impatiently tapped his fingers on his steering wheel. He was in a hurry. He had a lot to get done this afternoon.

Roslyn turned the lights on in the living room and checked the thermostat. Sixty degrees. "Come on in. You don't have to take off your shoes. Get a look at the view." She was standing in the living room of a three-bedroom ranch, her coat open over her gray pantsuit. A dark-complexioned man in his early thirties held the storm door open for his wife, a honey-blonde who was carrying their baby son wrapped in a blue-and-white checked blanket. Roslyn looked back down the hall at them. "The kitchen is to your left. The house has been well cared for. We'll go through it all, I'll fill you in on the particulars, but I thought you'd want to see the yard first."

They came through to the living room and looked out the picture window at the picket-fenced backyard and the view down to the lake. Two small boats bobbed in the distance. "The basement is a walkout, so it makes a great family room/play-room, and because of the drop in elevation, the fence doesn't obstruct the view."

The wife nodded. "How many bedrooms?"

"Three. And two baths. One in the hall and one in the master bedroom. Of course, the downstairs could be converted, too."

The husband looked at the polished light oak floors and ran his hand over the white painted trim of the doorway to the dining room. "Are all the floors wood?"

Roslyn nodded. "All oak and all beautifully finished, except downstairs. All the windows are double-glazed."

"What's the breaker box like?"

"We'll have a look in a minute. If you go through the door-way on the left, you'll see the dining room has the same great view." They walked into the dining room. A glass-topped table surrounded by eight chairs sat in the middle of the room. "I don't know if you like to entertain, but there's plenty of table room in here."

"The table included?" the husband asked.

"No. The owners are still in transition. So there's furniture in some of the rooms."

The wife carried the baby into the kitchen. The countertops were green and white ceramic tile and the cabinets matched the color of the oak floors. "The appliances are all pretty old."

"But they all work. And lots of people like to choose their own. The layout is solid, though. And the cabinets were custom built." Roslyn held out her hands. "Let me hold your son. You take a look in the cabinets."

"Okay."

Roslyn held the baby up on her shoulder and patted his back softly. His eyes were closed but his hand grabbed the lapel of her coat. Roslyn stood in place, lightly shifting weight from one foot to the other. The milky warm baby smell wafted up into her face. She felt like smiling. The mother opened and closed the cabinets and peered into the drawers. "Lots of space," Roslyn said.

The wife nodded. She turned to Roslyn and smiled. "Thanks." Roslyn handed the baby back. "The family room is downstairs?"

"Yeah, let's have a look. The breaker box and mechanicals are down there, too."

The basement was entirely open, except for two sets of steel support posts. To the far right, the breaker box hung on the wall close by the furnace and water heater. To the far left, an old oak desk, two tall metal file cabinets, and a huge old safe were arranged into a home office. "This will require some work just to make it safe," the wife said.

Roslyn slid open the patio door. "Right out into the yard."

The wife walked over and looked outside. There was a path trod down in the dirt along the back fence where a dog had run back and forth. The lawn was patchy in places. "I'm going to look at the bathrooms."

The husband was looking over the mechanicals. "I'll be up in a minute."

Ten minutes later, they were all standing in the driveway. "Lots of people are looking at this house," Roslyn said. "It's got a lot of potential and a great location."

"It needs some work. Maybe too much for us," the wife said.

"But you can move right in, make changes later when you know what you want. I can show you some places that look almost brand new inside, but to get a location like this, the price goes up dramatically."

"We'd still like to see a few," the husband said, "just to see how the price differential works."

"Call you later with some options?"

The husband and wife nodded.

After they got into their minivan and drove away, Roslyn stood in the driveway and called George. "You know that house on the lake where the owners have moved to Florida? There's a big old safe in the basement."

"Really? If they've already moved there's probably nothing in it."

"The house is still half-filled with furniture. And they moved down to a place they already owned. It could be a month before they come back to finish up."

"Okay. I'm game. By the way, a private investigator has been tailing Honeycutt, so I think he told you the truth."

"Tailing him?"

"Yeah. I picked her up this morning. Right now I'm prepping the package to spring on his wife."

"Are you sure about that?"

"How many more ten-thousand-dollar first of the months do you think there's going to be? If she found out about the affair, she'll find out about the blackmail. We're not putting your picture on the Internet. So this is our best chance for a bonus payment."

"Fair enough."

"Wish me luck."

"Luck."

George sat in the parking lot of Yoga Life Day Spa in a spot where he could watch the front door. A large line drawing of a smiling woman who was stretching like a cat was painted in black on the wall above the door. Billie's Audi sat between a metallic blue BMW and a white RAV to his right. Every couple of minutes, a few relaxed, rejuvenated women, chatting amiably and carrying gym bags or yoga mats, came out the doors. Finally, Billie came out, dressed in her usual business wear, carrying a pink and black gym bag. As she walked across the lot, George got out of his Avalon carrying a manila envelope that contained copies of the photos of Honeycutt and Roslyn. "Ms. Honeycutt. Ms. Honeycutt."

She stopped in the middle of the lot. "Do I know you?"

"No," George said. "We've never met. But we share a problem. I'm George Harrison. Roslyn's husband?"

Billie shook her head.

"Well, then I guess you're in for a shock. I received these this morning." He handed her the envelope.

She looked at the outside of the envelope, but she didn't open it.

"So you are familiar with the details."

"I don't know what you're talking about."

"Your husband is trying to wreck my marriage. I want you to keep that bastard away from my wife."

"Mr. Harrison, I know you're upset, but I don't know what you want me to do."

"Oh, is this the first time your husband's cheated on you? Let's see what Channel Eleven or the *Daily Gazette* have to say."

She dropped her gym bag on the pavement and clutched the mailer to her chest. "What do you want?"

He leaned in toward her. "I want that son of a bitch to stay away from my wife, and I want sixty thousand dollars so that I can take her away from here."

"Sixty thousand? Are you crazy?"

"You sound like you have a bad attitude, Ms. Honeycutt. Do you want me to go away quietly? Do you want to keep up your charade of being a happy couple?"

"I need some time."

"Take a good look at those photos. Two days to get the money or I go to the media." George started to walk away, and then turned on his heels. "Don't worry. I'll be in touch."

Billie started her car and turned on the heat. She set the envelope down in the passenger's seat. So the Harrisons were hoping to make money off Donald's stupidity. Though he'd used emotional language, George Harrison had seemed more calculating than angry. He was either a cold-blooded asshole — which would help to explain why his wife would run around on him — or it was a put-up job. What were the chances? Her eyes watered. Donald — as soon as his dick got hard there wasn't a drop of blood left in his brain. Every step of the way, this problem was becoming more complicated. She dabbed at her eyes with a tissue. Well, she wasn't going to be screwed over twice. She had to get out in front of the Harrisons, cause them to react to her rather than her reacting to them. She took out her phone and called Jessup.

"How can I help, Ms. Honeycutt?"

"Roslyn Harrison's husband George. I want him tracked."

"What are we looking for?"

"I don't trust him. I want to know where he goes."

"We talking human or GPS?"

"Let's start with GPS. He's driving a gold Avalon."

"We know where he lives. We'll have the tracker set before the end of the day."

Billie ended the call and searched her contacts for Bo's cell number. She looked at the screen of her smartphone and then closed her eyes and sat back in her seat. Maybe she was reading too much into this situation. She needed to talk to Bo in person so she could judge his reaction. She drove downtown. The sheriff's cruiser was parked in its spot at the back of the county jail. She parked in front in the visitor parking and went inside. The sergeant behind the counter buzzed her through and walked her back to Bo's office. "Please sit down. The sheriff will be with you in a minute. Coffee?"

"No thanks."

She sat down facing his desk. On her right was a wall of professional memorabilia: FBI courses, ATF citations, and State

Sheriff's Association awards. On her left were the personal photos of family vacations and fishing trips. A picture of his kids before his ex took them and moved away was under the glass top at the corner of his desk. Maybe he'd still have his family if he'd quit being sheriff. He could have come in with Tommy. But he didn't want to work for his brother. Didn't want to change their relationship. Couldn't blame him. She heard the door open behind her.

"Billie, how are you?"

She looked over her shoulder. "Hey, Bo."

He shut the door, came around his desk and sat down. "What's up?"

She told him about meeting George at Yoga Life Day Spa. He rubbed his chin. "So you think it's all a crock?"

She nodded.

"That would certainly let Donald off the hook, wouldn't it?"

"Not off the hook —"

"But mitigating circumstance. If he was set up by professionals."

"Exactly."

"But the husband didn't hold a gun to Donald's head while he had sex with the wife." He leaned forward. "See what I'm saying? They might be con artists, but you can't commit adultery with a man who won't sleep around. Factually, I'd say you're probably right about Donald being set up, but emotionally, Billie, it seems to me that you're grasping at straws."

"I have to admit, Bo, that when it comes to Donald I'm not thinking my straightest. But I really do think that he's learned his lesson this time. Will you help me with the Harrisons?"

"I'll scare them off. I just hope it gives you the result that you want."

"He drives a gold Avalon. I wrote down the plate number." She passed him a piece of notepaper. He picked up the desk phone. "Margaret? Can you run a plate for me?"

Billie stood up. "Thanks, Bo."

He gave her a wave good-bye while he held the receiver to his ear.

She walked out to her car. She had a missed call from Evelyn. She stood on the sidewalk in the sun in front of her car and called her back. "Evelyn. What can I do for you?"

"Billie. How are you?"

"I'm fine. What's up?"

"The Gilbert County sheriff is endorsing Kate Blackthorne."

"That's not surprising. I held out a little hope, but they're sort of cousins. They were raised together or something. What about the county executive for Gilbert?"

"It won't happen. The sheriff runs things over there. If we don't piss him off, we'll get their endorsement after we win the primary."

"Okay. So Pender County is all the more important to our rural strategy."

"You got it."

"Talk to you later."

George sat in line at the exit to the parking lot at the Buy-4-Less at Thackeray Place. The traffic on Thackeray Avenue pulsed out of the nearest intersections at odd intervals, blocking the exit, which seemed strange for the late afternoon when the traffic lights should have been timed, and the driver of the lead car, a minivan, seemed confused about how much space she needed to get out into traffic. A sheriff's deputy's cruiser drove by. Then another. The minivan turned right. The yellow Volvo in front of George was next. A gap opened up in the traffic and the Volvo jumped into the gap and sped off, immediately switching lanes. George glanced over his left shoulder at the oncoming traffic. There was space behind a black truck. He slipped easily into the space, drove two blocks, and turned into the neighborhood. His plan was to avoid the lights and the traffic and come up on his apartment complex from the golf course side. Even though he'd just gone to the grocery store, he was going to call Roslyn as soon as he got home and find out if she wanted to go to Café Mexicano. She didn't like to cook—except dessert—he didn't want to cook, and he wanted Mexican. He stopped at the four-way stop on the corner and turned left. Moments later, a sheriff's cruiser slid through the four-way without stopping, flipped on its lights, and came up onto his rear bumper. He pulled over in front of a light blue two-story with two grade-schoolers playing in the front yard.

A deputy sheriff got out of the cruiser and walked up to his window. The two kids, a boy and a girl, grass-stained jeans and old jackets, came up to about eight feet away and stood and watched. George lowered his window. "License and registration, sir."

"I'm going to get my license out of my wallet in my back pocket and the registration out of the glove box." George left the glove box door open and set his wallet in his lap. He handed the information to the deputy.

"Thank you."

"I didn't know the sheriff's department ran stops in the city limits."

"We can. It's in the county."

Another sheriff's department cruiser pulled up in front of George's Avalon. A man in a sheriff's department uniform wearing the nametag "SHERIFF TEARDALE" got out. "You can go on, Henry."

"Yes, sir." The deputy handed George's license and registration to the sheriff. Sheriff Teardale looked down into George's face without speaking until the deputy had driven off.

"George Harrison. Thought you died of lung cancer. Or was that one of your bandmates? You sure don't look much like your namesake."

George smiled softly. "How can I help you, Sheriff?"

"I put you in jail for a week and run this license hard, am I going to find anything interesting?"

"I don't think you can keep me over twenty-four hours without a charge."

Now it was the sheriff's turn to smile. "You're half right; you don't think. This is my county. Every inch of it. If I want you in jail, you're going to jail. If I want deputies following you everywhere you go, you'll be followed. So you can forget about that sixty thousand you were hoping to take off Billie Honeycutt and start packing. If there's one peep out of you, you'll live just long enough to regret it."

"You can't make me do anything."

"You've been watching too much TV. If I want you disappeared, you'll disappear. You and that slut you call a wife."

"Look, Sheriff, maybe I got off on the wrong foot here. I'm not wanting any trouble."

The sheriff tossed George's license and registration into his lap. "Exactly. So you're going to stop bothering Billie Honeycutt and her husband. You're going to say your good-byes, and you're going to head on down the road. Have a nice day." The sheriff got back in his cruiser, turned off his red lights, and drove away.

George sat for a moment. The two grade-schoolers kept right on sitting there in their yard, watching him as if they expected something else to happen. George put his registration back into the glove box and his license back into his wallet. It was beginning to appear that he and Roslyn had worn out their welcome. Bad luck that the Honeycutts were almost related to the sheriff. One more week until the money drop. If they kept their heads down, they could leave with that last ten thousand. George took out his phone and speed-dialed Roslyn. Then he glanced in his mirror to make sure no one was coming and pulled away from the curb.

The sheriff got in line at the Dairy Queen drive-through and took out his personal cell phone. "Billie? Got a minute? I believe I got your problem solved."

"So soon?"

"Yeah. He was acting a little pissy to begin with, but I convinced him as to the reality of his situation."

"Still look like a setup?"

"He was a mighty cool customer. He didn't get out his crying towel. So, yeah, probably a setup."

"How long until they're gone?"

"Could be a few days or so, but they won't bother you anymore."

"Thanks, Bo."

The sheriff pulled up to the outside menu.

"Welcome to Dairy Queen. Can I take your order?"

"Chocolate malted with extra malt."

"Pull up to the second window."

George and Roslyn sat at a window booth in Café Mexicano. The dining room was about three-quarters full, mostly families with younger kids. It was dark outside, and the window reflected their images back at them. Roslyn was picking at her enchiladas con mole, with a side of vegetarian beans and a salad. George was eating his third taco. He hadn't touched his salsa-topped rice or his refried beans. He put down his taco, sipped his Coke, and looked at her plate. "Something wrong with your food?"

"Spices taste weird."

George reached across the table with his fork, snagged a bit of enchilada, and dipped it into the sauce. "Same as always. Just a touch too much onion for me."

She made a face. "I guess my tummy is a little off."

"You coming down with something?"

"I feel fine."

"Maybe we should postpone."

"I'll eat the salad and beans. This could be our last opportunity if the sheriff starts watching us."

"You're right about that."

After they finished eating, they went home and changed into some breaking-and-entering clothes: black jeans and turtlenecks with dark-colored jackets. George shouldered their work daypack, which contained everything they might need for this sort of job—flashlights, latex gloves, lock picks, roll-up nylon bag, can of spray paint, glass cutter. George set the daypack into the back seat floor of the Avalon before he got into the driver's seat. "All set, honey?"

"We taking your car or picking up something along the way?"

"The house is isolated and empty. There're no surveillance cameras, right?"

"Not even an alarm system. Nothing but old-school trust protecting the safe in the basement."

"Why risk picking up a car?"

They drove out to Lakeview Estates, the original large lot subdivision just outside of Randal Junction, where Roslyn had shown the ranch on the lake earlier that day. The streetlights were well spaced. Every house sat in its own pool of light. With so little light cast about at ground level, the night sky was huge with stars. George pulled the Avalon up at the bottom of the driveway under a tall Ponderosa pine shielded by overgrown yew bushes. He handed latex gloves to Roslyn before he put on his own. "No fence?"

"Gate on the left."

They walked down the edge of the concrete drive, outside the perimeter of light shining from the spotlights in front of the house, and down the steps at the side of the garage, through the wooden gate in the picket fence, and into the backyard, George leading the way with a small flashlight. "Anyone show the house after you?"

"You think we'd be standing here if I was the last one in?"

George picked the lock on the patio door. "Here we go."

The door slid half an inch and stopped. "Someone engaged the security bolt."

"Didn't have one. Must be a dowel."

"Let's try the garage."

They walked back up the hill at the side of the house. The side window to the garage was just out of reach. They looked around in the dark. Roslyn noticed an old steel trashcan just beyond the gate in the wooden fence. They crept down to it and looked inside. Empty. They left the lid, carried the trashcan back up to the window, and flipped it over. George climbed up on it. He glanced over his shoulder. He couldn't see any light at the neighbors'. It was too early in the year for open windows. He got the glasscutter out of the daypack, cut an "X" into the lower glass of the double-hung window, and whacked it with his elbow. The glass gave a sharp crack. He hit it again. Glass fell into the garage. He reached in, unlocked the latch, and pushed the window open. Once in the garage, he picked the lock to the kitchen door. The first floor was lit up, but just as Roslyn had indicated, there was no evidence of an alarm system. They went downstairs and turned on the basement lights. George looked at the safe and smiled. "When they build these things, customers thought if the safe was big and heavy, it would be hard to break into. What a joke."

A few minutes later, George had the safe open. Inside, they found a file folder of documents, including a deed, two wills, and some insurance policies; a stack of savings bonds; a binder of old coins; and a shoebox of cash. George shook his head. "Is there a businessman in this town who isn't skimming profits to avoid taxes?"

He passed the money back to Roslyn, then shoved the empty shoebox and everything else back inside.

"What about the coins?"

"They're just evidence we don't want to be caught with." He locked the safe. "Let's get out of here."

While George and Roslyn were parking in front of the house in Lakeview Estates, Jessup sat in his office putting stamps on some billing statements that he wanted to get into the mail tomorrow. This last week had been very successful. With any luck, there would be a few more dollars destined for the Honeycutt account. He turned to his computer and accessed the GPS tracker on Honeycutt's car. The Cadillac was parked in the garage for the night. He switched to Harrison's car. It had gone from Café Mexicano, back to his apartment, and now out to Lakeview Estates. What was going on? Was Harrison in his car or was it his wife? And what was Honeycutt driving? Cindi had gone home for the evening after she'd tucked Honeycutt in. So there were no eyes on him. Jessup tapped his pencil on his desk. Plain paranoia or moneymaking opportunity? Why not roll the dice? He got in his Bronco and drove out to Lakeview Estates, where he let the GPS guide him to Harrison's Avalon, hidden behind some bushes at a for-sale house. He cut off his lights, got out his camera, and waited. Five minutes later, he saw two people dressed in black, sneaking down the driveway in the shadows, a small beam of light illuminating their path. He got out of his truck, gripped his right hand around the hammerless .38 revolver in his jacket pocket, and held his camera ready to shoot in his left. Just as the two people reached the car, he popped out of the bushes, took three pictures in quick succession, the flash going off like a strobe, and pulled the gun from his pocket. "Keep your hands where I can see them."

The two people turned on their heels.

"If you run, I shoot."

They turned back around with their hands up. Jessup stepped closer. "Well, well, George and Roslyn Harrison."

"Who are you?" George asked.

"Stan Jessup."

"And why are you following us?"

"What are you doing out here?"

"We're real estate agents. We're just getting some night time pictures of the property."

"Expect me to believe that?"

"Could you stop pointing that gun at us?"

"Slip off that backpack and hand it to her. Ms. Harrison, why don't you step up to the back of the car and empty out that bag on the trunk lid?"

"We don't have to cooperate with you," George said.

"I've got two hands. I can set down the camera and call the sheriffs and still point this gun."

"Maybe we can reach an accommodation."

"Maybe we can."

George handed Roslyn the daypack. She stepped up to the trunk lid and slowly set their tools out of the bag.

"Shine the light on it," Jessup said.

George moved the beam onto the trunk lid.

"Very incriminating," Jessup said. "Where's the rest of it? It's a bit cold for a strip search."

Roslyn set the four bundles of cash on the trunk lid and held the daypack upside down and shook it.

"Step back."

Roslyn stepped back to George. Jessup moved up to the trunk lid and eyed the money. "Not bad for a few hours' work. I believe one of these is mine. Sound fair to you?"

"Plus the pictures."

"You familiar with cameras?"

George nodded.

Jessup held out the camera. "Delete the pictures yourself. Just don't get in too big a hurry. We still have trust issues."

George took the camera from Jessup and deleted the pictures.

"Satisfied?"

"Yeah. Here's your camera." George passed it to him. "Relax, I'm not willing to get shot over a few dollars. Don't need the trouble and don't need the police."

"That sounds like a wise policy." Jessup put the gun in his pocket and picked up one of the bundles. "So now you know you're being tailed. Enjoy your evening."

Roslyn put the tools and the three remaining bundles of money back into the daypack, while George watched Jessup's taillights disappear at the turn at the end of the block. Then they got into the Avalon and drove off in the opposite direction. "I knew Honeycutt's wife was having him followed. I didn't know she was having you followed as well."

"Was it me?" Roslyn replied. "Or did she put Jessup on you after you asked her for the sixty grand?"

"Fair point." George turned right onto the highway.

"Left is quicker."

"I know. I'm taking the stupidest way back home. I don't want any more surprises."

"When do we leave?"

"Next week is the first of the month. I still think we should wait until we collect that last ten thousand. As long as we keep our heads down we should be all right. Show some houses. Go to the movies. Stay away from Honeycutt and his wife."

"It's been a good little run."

"Yes, it has."

Jessup rang the doorbell to the Honeycutts' house. Why did she call wanting to see him so late? It couldn't be good. Good news from clients came during business hours. Was she feeling guilty for investigating her husband? The injured party often felt it was their fault for finding out the truth, but that didn't seem in character for Billie Honeycutt. Had she just decided she had enough information? That it was time to pull the plug? Jessup steeled himself for the bad news. Billie answered the door herself. She was still dressed from her workday in a gray skirt suit, light blue shirt, and jade pendant. "You wanted to see me in person, ma'am?"

"Thanks for stopping by so late, Stan." She glanced up the stairs. "Why don't you come on in? I'll only keep you a minute." She led him into the living room, but she didn't ask him to sit down. "Care for a drink?"

"No, thanks, ma'am." There was a fire going in the white marble fireplace. A hardcover book lay open on the end table by a sage green wingback chair.

"Anything new to report?"

He slipped a toothpick into the side of his mouth. "Nothing. The Harrisons have been together all evening." He took out his notebook and pretended to look at his notes. "According to the GPS log, they went from home to Café Mexicano. Then back home. Stayed in."

"You saw them yourself?"

"Yes, ma'am. Just to make sure the GPS was working, I drove over to the restaurant. They were together."

"What's she look like?"

He looked up at her face. "You've never seen her?"

She wouldn't meet his eyes. "The pictures—I only glanced at them."

He shrugged. He looked her over as he spoke. "She's about your height, similar build, same hair color. She dresses up well."

Billie glanced in the antique mirror on the wall over the drinks cabinet.

Jessup took the toothpick out of his mouth. "But not as well as you."

Billie sighed. "Take your associate off of Donald. Leave the GPS. Put your associate on Roslyn Harrison."

"I could cover them both, if you like."

"No, cover the Harrison woman. With the political season heating up, we don't want anyone to find out that a private investigator has been following Donald. We've taken enough chances."

"What hours do you want?"

"It should only be a few more days, and eight to five should be enough. Donald's at home in the evening."

"Only a few more days?"

"A reliable source had promised me that the Harrisons are leaving town."

"I see. So we're continuing with the GPS on Donald and Harrison, and we'll put eyes on his wife. We'll get started first thing in the morning." Jessup put the toothpick back in his mouth. "Anything else?"

She shook her head. "Thank you, Stan."

6: The Unexpected Complication

The next morning, Roslyn was on her knees in her underwear in front of the toilet, holding her hair back with one hand, vomiting. George, already in suit and tie, poked his head in the door and turned on the bathroom fan. "You okay?"

"Yeah, I'm fine."

He crouched down beside her and put his hand on her shoulder. "You don't sound fine."

"I'm okay."

"Want me to make you a doctor's appointment?"

"Georgie, I'm sure I'll be okay in a minute."

"If you're sure, I've got to get going."

"I'm sure."

"Call me if you need me."

He stood up and left. Roslyn got up, rinsed her mouth at the sink, and brushed her teeth. What was the date? When was her last period? But that was crazy thinking. Her period hadn't been regular in a couple of years. She went into the bedroom, picked up her smartphone off of the dresser, and pulled up her personal calendar. Almost six weeks. Crazy thinking. Must be something else. She was having trouble at supper last night. What about yesterday lunch? Yogurt and a pack of cheese crackers. She made a cup of mint tea to settle her stomach and got dressed for the day: charcoal pantsuit, white scoop-necked blouse, stained-glass window silk scarf looped around her throat. She looked in the mirror. Voilà, real estate agent. What was the weather going to be? Warm for March. She put on her lined raincoat. She was showing a house in an hour. Her plan was to go into the office and act like an actual real estate agent until it was time to meet her new clients, but as she drove by the Shop-N-Save Grocery megastore she pulled into the parking lot and went into the pharmacy.

She stood in the aisle looking at the huge selection of over-the-counter heartburn meds, selected a few at random, and read the information on the boxes, but she wasn't convinced they would help with her nausea. Then she turned to the vitamins: multi, multi for women, multi for older women. What brand did she used to take? All she could remember was the red box. She drifted by the nutritional supplements — diet drinks, whey powder, glucosamine — and found herself in front of the shelves that contained the pregnancy tests, which were located next to the condoms and spermicides straight across from the pharmacy counter. There were three brands of pregnancy tests, but she didn't bother to read the boxes. It was a crazy idea, impossible, so far outside the realm of the probable that it was a joke. She felt like a middle-schooler about to shoplift a CD. She glanced around as if she were afraid she was being watched. She looked over at the next shelf. Eye drops. She gave the pregnancy tests one last sidelong glance, picked up one at random, and stepped up to the pharmacy counter. She paid without looking at the clerk, declined a bag, and slipped the test into her handbag.

Later, after she'd wasted two and a half hours on an obsessive-compulsive couple who wanted a McMansion for the price of a fixer-upper, she drove home. The test was weighing on her mind, like junky drugs just bought on a street corner. She sat on the sofa, tore open one end of the box, and read the directions slowly, twice. Collect a urine sample in the little cup. Uncover the sensor tip on the digital test stick and dip it into the urine for twenty seconds. Wait a few minutes for the readout to say "pregnant" or "not pregnant." She got up, went into the kitchen and made a cup of English breakfast tea. She added a little milk and two teaspoons of sugar. She stood at the kitchen counter stirring the tea, occasionally looking at the open box and the instructions lying on the coffee table in the living room. Finally, she set the spoon down and sipped the tea. She should just throw the test away. She was grasping at straws. If she were still sick tomorrow, she should go to the urgent care clinic.

She set her teacup down. She leaned on the counter and closed her eyes. She saw nothing. It was nothing. There was nothing to be afraid of. Her mind was clear. She picked up the test from the coffee table, went into the bathroom, squatted over the toilet, and collected the urine sample in the little cup. She set the little cup on the sink counter, finished up, and then dipped the test stick into it. She left the test stick in the bathroom. Waste of time. She went back to her cup of tea and microwaved it for twenty seconds. She had to be wrong. Had to be. She'd been pregnant once, a long time ago. She knew what it felt like and this wasn't it. She got her tea out of the microwave and sipped it. She went back into the bathroom and read the display on the test stick. "Pregnant." Christ. She went into the living room, circled the coffee table like a cat, and looked at the display again. She hadn't misread it. She picked up the directions and scanned through them, rereading the important words. She was forty-four years old. It just wasn't possible. George couldn't have kids. He'd had a vasectomy years ago. She wasn't on the pill, but Honeycutt always wore a condom. She made sure of that. God. She looked at the display again. She picked up her phone. "George? I need you right now. I'm at home."

What was George going to say? How angry was he going to be? She paced back and forth from the living room through the kitchen, opened the refrigerator, found nothing she wanted to eat, closed it, looked in the pantry, got out a loaf of whole wheat bread, opened it, got out a slice, changed her mind, and put it back in the bag. She still had half a cup of tea sitting on the counter. She drank it cold.

George burst through the front door. "Okay. What's the crisis? You still sick? We going to the clinic?"

She took a deep breath. "Sit down." She pointed at the sofa.

"Roz, I pushed a client out of a house."

"Sit."

He sat on the sofa, but he didn't take his eyes off of her. She stood behind the chair closest to the kitchen and gripped the back in her hands. "I'm pregnant."

George's mouth fell open. "Pregnant?"

She nodded. "Yeah, I think so."

"The throwing up? Could be lots of things."

"I took a test." She pointed to the test stick on the coffee table.

He picked it up and read the display. "Wouldn't do me any good to read the instructions?"

She shook her head "no."

He set the test stick back down.

She smiled a crooked, broken smile. "The last hurrah. Who knew?"

He stood up. "It's no problem, Roz. We've got the cash. We're still early, right? We'll get this little problem squared away."

"You're not mad at me?"

"Mad? Why? Come on, I know you took every precaution." He studied her. "Have I ever hurt you? Come on, you aren't afraid of me, are you?" He went to her and hugged her and patted her back.

"I don't know what I was thinking," she said.

"Sit down. This is a solvable problem. This morning's just been a little too crazy for you. I'll make you some lunch. You relax." He walked her to the sofa. Then he went back into the kitchen, got plates from the cabinet, and put bread on the plates for sandwich making. "Hummus or cheese? I think that's all we have."

"Hummus."

He got hummus, lettuce and mayonnaise out of the fridge, spread the mayo and the hummus. "How about olives?"

"Not for me."

He put on the lettuce, put on the top slice of bread, and cut the sandwich corner to corner. "Milk?"

"Okay."

He brought her a sandwich and a glass of milk. He had a manic look in his eye. On his way back into the kitchen to get his sandwich, he spun on his heels and stared down at her.

"What is it?" she said. "Why are you looking at me like that?"

"You know, this might sound a little over the top, but hear me out." He laughed. "You're carrying Honeycutt's baby. He's running for Congress. What do you think they would pay to hush that up? We could get, what? Something well north of a hundred thousand?"

"But George—I don't know—how long would I have to be pregnant?"

"They pay; we deal with the problem."

"Easy for you to say. You're not the one growing and changing."

"We're talking days, not weeks. Days. Just give it a try. You can blow the whistle whenever you want. You'll be in charge."

"You really mean that?"

"Absolutely. You can go to a clinic without ever talking to me about it again. But before you jump in the car, just think about it. We could be off work a long, long time. And it's not like they don't have it coming. Adulterers, election riggers, over-entitled selfish assholes. Right? Let's make our play. Work this for a couple of days. They panic, pay off, and *poof*, we're gone."

"I don't know, Georgie. I don't know. This is all so weird."

"Just think about it, Roz. Eat your lunch. Rest. Let it percolate."

Earlier, when Roslyn had been standing in the pharmacy aisle looking at the pregnancy tests, Cindi had been watching her from the end of the row, acting as if she were choosing among the vast selection of body lotions. It never ceased to amaze her that no one noticed the full-figure, middle-aged black woman. It was like she wasn't young enough to be a shoplifter, and she wasn't important enough to rate a "can I help you, ma'am?" She was completely invisible. She watched Roslyn pay for the pregnancy test and shove it down into her handbag. Then she followed her out of the Shop-N-Save and tailed her around town until they made their way back to her apartment. She parked in a visitor's spot in the apartment parking lot just in sight of Roslyn's car, where she was sitting when Harrison came flying into the parking lot, pulled in beside Roslyn's car and ran up to their apartment. She called Jessup.

"Are you serious?" She could hear him getting up out of his chair. "No mistake?"

"I was close enough to read the label."

"You are the best. I'd kiss you if you were here. Stay on her. I'm going to go see Ms. Honeycutt."

"That will be an interesting conversation."

"The trick is to turn it from a meltdown to a bonus."

"Good luck."

Jessup sat back down at his desk. This was a delicate situation. He needed to see Ms. Honeycutt in person if he were going to work this information to the best advantage. On the phone, she could hang up, go cry, start hating on the messenger. He couldn't have that. He rubbed his hands together. He needed to frame the situation so that she would be grateful for his initiative. He picked up the phone and called her. The call flipped over to her voice mail. "Ms. Honeycutt, please call me at my cell." He hung up. He taped a "back in thirty minutes" note on the glass door, locked up, and walked down the strip mall to Cosmo's Barbeque and Bagels. He really shouldn't have a big lunch, but he felt like a celebration. The noon rush was over, so there was no line to order and only half the red-and-white checked Formica tables were occupied. In only a few minutes he was sitting at a window table eating a pork barbeque sandwich with a side of coleslaw. He was halfway through his sandwich when Billie returned his call.

"What's so urgent?"

Jessup wiped his mouth with a napkin. "I've got some information I need to share with you in person."

"Just tell me."

"I really need to tell you in person. Besides, I'm standing in a public place and this info is confidential. Where are you? I can come to you."

She sighed. "No, that's okay. I'll meet you at your office in fifteen minutes."

Jessup turned off his phone. He took one more bite of barbeque, wrapped the remainder of the sandwich in a napkin, and dumped his tray on his way to the door. He was sitting behind his desk when Billie arrived. He stood up when he saw her come through the front door. "Come on back."

Billie walked past the orange cubicles in the front and into his private office. "So what's the big secret?"

"Maybe you want to sit down."

"Look, Stan, I'm in a hurry, so let's get to it."

"Okay. Cindi, my operative, was tailing Roslyn Harrison this morning."

Billie shrugged. "So?"

"She followed her into a pharmacy."

"Yeah?"

"Well, this might be nothing, but she watched her buy a pregnancy test."

"Pregnancy test?"

Jessup nodded.

Billie sat down. She looked down at her shoes. She took a few breaths. Then she looked up at Jessup. "But she's a married woman."

"That's true."

"Just because she might be pregnant doesn't mean it's Donald's."

"Also true." Jessup rubbed his mustache with his index finger. "The problem isn't what's true or not true. The problem is what the wrong kind of people might infer."

"Your operative—Cindi. She couldn't be mistaken?"

Jessup shook his head. "She was standing as close as we are now."

Billie nodded thoughtfully. Her eyes teared up. Why did she have to be a crier? Stan pushed a box of tissue across the desk toward her. She blotted her eyes. She wasn't going to break down. Again. Not in front of Stan. Pregnant. Donald knew just how to hurt her even when he didn't mean to. She couldn't have children. Tommy didn't care, but it had almost been a deal breaker with Donald. Was that why he couldn't keep his pants zipped? God, how had her life suddenly become such a soap opera? She was still a desirable woman. She was rich. Anyone she wanted to would sleep with her. Somehow she'd saddled herself with a man who just couldn't seem to see who she was. Why had she done that? Why was she in love with a man who only wanted to hurt her? What did it say about her if that was the kind of man she was drawn to? And George Harrison had already asked her for money. What if he decided to use the pregnancy to blackmail her?

She needed to empty her mind. Think about something else. The pregnancy test kit didn't mean anything. Roslyn Harrison wasn't pregnant. Bo had taken care of her husband. Billie took a deep breath. Speculating would only make her crazy. She wasn't a basket case. She wasn't attracted to abusers. She deserved to be loved for who she was. She looked up at Stan, who was leaning over his desk with a concerned expression on his face. She preferred men with hair, though that hadn't bothered her with Tommy. She stood up. "Have sex with me."

Jessup had a look on his face like his hearing wasn't trustworthy. "What?"

"Sex. Right here. Right now."

"Ms. Honeycutt, don't get me wrong. You're a good-looking woman. But I don't think your mind is right. You need to calm down, have something to drink, think things through."

She pulled off her suit jacket, tossed it on the chair, and started unbuttoning her blouse. She wouldn't be getting back at Donald. He wouldn't even care. "Call me Billie."

"This is a bad idea, Ms. Honeycutt."

She pulled her blouse out of the top of her skirt, hiked up the skirt, and shoved her thumbs under the tops of her pantyhose and panties.

"To hell with it," Jessup said. "I'm locking the door."

7: The Hard Game

At 8:00 a.m. the next morning Honeycutt reached in the center console for his sunglasses as he drove east across town against the morning traffic. He was going to meet Roslyn at the Hillside Motel. He didn't know why. He'd promised Billie that he would never see Roslyn again. But when she called he just couldn't seem to help himself. It had only been three days since he'd broken off with her, but he missed her. He enjoyed just being in the same room with her. With Roslyn there were never any demands or pressure to do a particular thing; he could just be himself. And it didn't help that Billie was being cold to him. Putting him in the guest bedroom. That was bullshit. But, no matter what she did, he wasn't going to break his promise to her and have sex with Roslyn. Billie was his number one. She'd been right to be angry with him. Especially after Roslyn's husband had demanded money. He certainly hadn't seen that coming. He'd let his relationship with Roslyn get out of hand, but that was over. He'd learned his lesson. He was going to win back Billie's trust.

He looked in his rearview mirror. No one was following him. He turned off the highway into the motel parking lot. That morning, before he left the house, he'd searched the car for tracking devices. The car was clean. No one could be following him. And his alibi was solid. If Billie called the health spa, Art would say he was in the sauna. He saw Roslyn's red Lincoln parked in front of one of the black doors on the backside of the building, pulled in beside it, and knocked on the door.

Roslyn opened the door. Her hair hung down on her shoulders. She was wearing a black long-sleeve T-shirt with red satin piping, gray yoga pants, and running shoes. She stepped to the side to let him come in and then shut the door behind him. "How have you been?"

"Really?" he asked. "I've been suffering. Billie's been making me pay. But that's what I deserve."

She stepped toward him. He backed away and held his hands up, palm out. "I promised Billie that I wouldn't sleep with you anymore. I'm here for you, but just as a friend." He glanced about the room. The faded drapes, worn-down carpet, and scratched furniture seemed depressing in a way they never had before. "So, what's this all about?"

"Okay," she nodded her head. She went over to her handbag on the bed and got out the pregnancy test stick. She brought it back to where he stood by the door and held it up. "I'm going to have a baby."

He craned forward, trying to read the display without taking the test stick out of her hand. "You're lying."

"Are you afraid to hold it? Take it." She pushed the test stick into his hand. It fell on the carpet. "Pick it up."

He picked up the test stick and read the display. Pregnant. "Is this really yours?"

"Whose else would it be?"

He read it again. "How do you know it's not George?"

"George can't have kids. He had a vasectomy a long time ago."

He tossed the test stick at her. She caught it after it bounced off her chest. "I don't believe you," he said.

She held the test stick in her left fist. Her lower lip trembled. He grabbed her by the arms and shook her. "What's your game? George already knows, doesn't he? This is nothing but a scam. You're not pregnant. It's all a load of crap."

"No!" she yelled. "I'm pregnant. It's your baby. You can hurt me, but that's not going to change anything."

He stopped still, his hands squeezing her wrists. "My baby?"
She nodded.

"Really?" He studied her face. "My God, I think maybe you are telling the truth." He pushed her away. "My baby." Then he reached for her. She flinched and took a step back. "No, no, no." He grabbed her by the shoulders. She started to struggle. "I'm so sorry." He pulled her close. "So sorry." He kissed her neck. "Don't you do anything crazy. I'm going to take care of you. My baby. You're having my baby." He kissed her eyes and her cheeks.

"Let go," she said. "Let go." She squirmed out of his arms. She couldn't believe what she was hearing. "You want the baby?"

"Of course I want my baby." He took her hands in his and looked her in the eyes. "We'll figure this out. I promise."

"What about Billie? What about the election?"

"The most important thing right now is taking care of you and making sure the baby is healthy. Everything else can work itself out."

She put her arms around his neck. "Make love to me. Make love to me right now."

He kissed her. She loosened his tie and started unbuttoning his shirt. He took off his suit coat, tossed it onto a chair, picked her up, and carried her to the bed. She crawled up the bed to the pillows, rolled over on her back, and pulled off her yoga pants. Without taking his eyes off her, he kicked off his shoes and took off his suit pants. Then he joined her on the king-size bed, took her gently in his arms, and kissed her lovingly before he pulled her T-shirt off over her head. Afterward, cuddling in the middle of the bed, he asked her, "Boy or girl?"

"I don't care."

He stroked her face. "I really would like a son, but I'd be happy with a daughter, I know it."

"So what do we do now?"

"I have to talk with Billie. Make her see reason. Get with her and Evelyn to see how we work the campaign."

"How mad do you think she's going to be?"

"It's going to take two or three conversations. But trust me, she wants me happy. She'll come around just as soon as she sees it won't jeopardize the election."

Jessup sat in an old white Dodge Dakota truck with a gray camper top at the far side of the potholed back parking lot of the Hilltop Motel, drinking coffee from a takeout cup and listening to the morning drive show on the country station. He'd followed Roslyn there and had watched Honeycutt go into the room. The door opened. Honeycutt came out, grinning and adjusting his tie. Jessup slid down in the seat, counted to twenty, sat back up, and watched Honeycutt drive away. He sipped his coffee and listened to the weather report, sunny and mid-sixties, before he called Billie. "Ms. Honeycutt? I was tracking Roslyn this morning."

Billie sat at the kitchen island, looking out at the birdfeeder in the backyard. A blue jay had just shooed off a smaller bird. "If it's bad news, don't string it out."

"Donald met her at the Hilltop Motel. Didn't even try to hide. He was in the room about an hour."

Roslyn stood in the narrow, mold-stained shower of the motel room, her hair covered by a plastic shower cap. Who would have thought that he would want the baby? It was something she surely hadn't thought about. Having the baby. Being a mother. A mom. A little person holding her leg, saying "I love you" and always meaning it. A shiver ran down her spine. A vulnerable little person to lie to and betray. Just like her lying bitch mother had done. The water was going cold. She turned the controller toward "hot." It was a stupid, crazy idea. Not possible for her. What would George say? She put her hands on her belly. She could have the baby, stay here with Donald, start a new life. But then she'd always be at his mercy. It would never work. She didn't deserve a baby. She couldn't keep it and be who she was. She should have asked Donald for money. That was what she was supposed to do; she should have just gotten it done. But she hadn't expected him to be happy. She turned off the water and reached for the thin, gray towel. She needed to stay focused on who she was and the life she'd chosen. Her and George. It was the only life she knew and she was too old to start over.

Honeycutt stood in the sunlight in the family room, holding a cup of coffee in his hand. Billie stood between the granite kitchen counter and the family room sofa. "Mamie," she said, "could you go upstairs and help the girls in the bedrooms?"

"Yes, ma'am." Mamie stopped rinsing the breakfast dishes and loading the dishwasher. She turned off the tap, laid her yellow rubber gloves over the edge of the sink, and headed for the stairs in the front hall.

Honeycutt shrugged. "I guess we're going to get loud."

Billie spun on her heels. Yesterday's meeting with Jessup was cascading through her mind. *Please, God, not that. Don't let it be the worst.* "What do you think?" she hissed. "You gave me your word. No bimbos until after the election. You broke it. Then you promised to give up this woman. The man I've got following her finds you with her at the no-tell motel. I'm not supposed to feel betrayed? I should have you sprayed for bugs before I let you in the house."

"Billie, really, it's not like it appears. I know I look like a worthless, sorry asshole, but I've got amazing news."

"I can't believe you're trying to sell this." She gripped the sofa to steady herself. *Please, God, don't let that woman be pregnant.*

Honeycutt set his coffee down on the end table at the end of the sofa. "I know; I know you're angry. Just listen. Listen with an open mind. Can you do that? Take a deep breath. I'm committed to you. I'm committed to our plans. We're going to win in the fall. We're going to Washington, DC. Just take a deep breath."

She inhaled and exhaled slowly. "Okay, I'm waiting."

He smiled. "I'm going to be a father."

She launched herself across the space between them, screaming, and beat on him with her fists, yelling and hitting him as he backed across the room, blocking her fists with his arms and trying to get a word in, until he tripped over a leg to the coffee table and fell back on the carpet. She kicked at his thigh, tears streaming down her face. "Why don't you just murder me — cut my throat — no, poison's more your style." She lay down on the sofa in the fetal position and sobbed.

"Bils, baby, I've got everything under control. I'm turning Roslyn to our side." He knelt down beside her, hoping to comfort her.

"Don't you touch me."

Honeycutt went to the kitchen, poured a glass of water, and brought it back to her. "Drink some water. Blow your nose. I know this seems bad to you."

She sat up and took the glass. "Bad? Donald, this is a nuclear-bomb-level clusterfuck. I can't even put my mind around how you could be happy." She took a drink. "Do you love her?"

"It's my baby."

"How do you know it's yours?"

"George can't have kids."

"Says who?" She set the glass on the coffee table and blotted her face with a wad of tissues. "You're living in a fantasy right now. I get that. But you need to back up two steps. How much money does she want?"

"She didn't ask me for any money."

"So she's playing it cool. We'll pay for the abortion and a parting gift—say, twenty, thirty thousand, if she keeps her mouth shut and leaves the state."

"Billie, you're not listening. I want this baby."

"Are you insane?"

"Let's pray about this."

"It's a little late to fall back on Jesus, don't you think? We've got plans. You won't make it through the primary carrying a baby momma."

"Okay, the cover up is a heavy lift, but hear me out. We hide her away, set up a cover story of a surrogate just in case—everyone knows you can't have kids—adopt the baby after the election. Roslyn goes on her way. We keep the baby and raise it as ours. This mess isn't the baby's fault. Can we at least agree on that?"

"Raise the baby as ours? You really think you can sell Roslyn on this? Thus far, it looks like she's been playing you."

"If she's after money, this is how she's going to get it. Where else is she going to turn? Who'll pay as much as us?"

Billie held up one hand for quiet and looked out the back-yard windows. She should just give up her dream of being a congressman's wife and file for divorce. Donald was way beyond high maintenance. He was making her crazy. Sex with Jessup had been a stupid mistake and it hadn't even made her feel better. Donald was always going to find a way to make her cry. She should cut her losses and find a man who wanted to make her happy. How hard could it be? She sighed. She just couldn't do it. She didn't know why, but she just couldn't let him go. "This is what I'm willing to do. We take her to my cousin Natalie—"

"Your OB/GYN?"

She nodded. "I'll make an appointment as if it's for me. We make sure she's pregnant; make sure she's healthy; find out when we can determine paternity."

"I knew you'd understand, Bils. I knew you'd understand. We can make this work."

"Donny, don't read into what I've said. If the baby is really yours; then I'll think hard about the next step."

Honeycutt knelt down to hug her. She pushed him away. "You smell like her. I'm mad at you. I have a right to be mad at you. I don't want you touching me."

"Okay, Bils, okay."

"You need to think about how you're going to make this up to me and win back my trust."

"Everything is going to be perfect, honey; just wait and see. This time next year, you'll be the happiest woman in Washington, DC."

Billie strode into the campaign office. Six college-age interns, two men and four women, were sitting around the gray metal desks in the front office, talking on phones or working on computers. Billie nodded and waved her way through, knocked on Evelyn's open door, and closed the door behind her. Evelyn, sitting at her old oak desk with her long gray-brown braid hanging over her left shoulder and a phone up against her right ear, glanced up from her phone call and motioned toward the armchair facing her desk. "Okay," she said. "Okay. Thanks." She hung up the phone, took off her reading glasses, and let them hang from a chain around her neck.

"Billie, I wasn't expecting you. I've got another appointment in fifteen minutes."

"We've got a problem."

Evelyn looked from Billie's face to the closed door and back. "Really? That kind of problem? He swore he'd keep his pants zipped up."

"I know. You can't be more disappointed than me."

"Damn it, Billie, you swore you'd make sure he stayed off the extracurricular."

"I know."

"That's been the whole basis of my involvement."

"You think I like sitting here?"

"You know how I feel about this sort of thing. Once you start covering up, there's no turning back and there's no guarantee the truth won't come out at the worst possible time."

"Sit back, take a deep breath, and let me fill you in on where we're at." Billie told Evelyn everything she knew about Roslyn and George, including the blackmail demand. As Billie spoke, the color drained from Evelyn's face.

The phone rang. Evelyn picked it up. Without waiting to hear who it was, she said, "I'll have to call you back." She laid the receiver gently into the cradle. "I guess I should tell the interns and draft a statement for the press. We'll call it—what? Sudden illness? No, withdrawing from the race for private family reasons. That sounds better. And we'll start a rumor about some sort of curable cancer. That way, in two years he can try again if this situation doesn't blow up in your faces."

"Evelyn, I know what you're going through right now. I was going through it an hour ago. Just hear me out. We've got a lot invested in this campaign. We've got this one problem. I know it's not little, but it's only one. I've got PIs on it. We contain it; bag it up tight; get everyone on the same page. The Harrisons get paid; they don't want to rock the boat. That's the kind of people they are."

Evelyn pulled gently on her braid. "Think about it. She'll be three months along at the June primary. Depending on how she carries the baby, we might be able to hide it or at least avoid video evidence. In November, though, she'll be as big as a house or carrying the kid in her arms."

"All of this could go away in the next few weeks."

"You think Donald will change his mind? You know you're talking crazy."

"You got another job to go to?"

"This race is over."

"Donald screwed up. And I screwed up by letting him. But we're not done, Evelyn. You got involved in this race because you need a win. You want to claw your way back into the game. So put your game face on and do what you promised to do."

"You're not going to guilt-trip me." She closed her eyes and rubbed her temples. When she opened her eyes, she leaned over her desk and looked hard into Billie's face. "You want to roll the dice? Okay. Suit yourself. We didn't have this conversation. I don't know anything about this problem. It gets away from you and I'm gone. The press release will tell just how shocked I am. I'm not leaving my reputation on the floor with your broken dreams. That's the best I can do."

"Thank you, Evelyn. You're making the right decision. I'm getting this thing cleared up as we speak. You'll never hear a peep about it."

Roslyn and George stood at the granite-topped kitchen peninsula in their apartment, the lunch dishes still on the counter. George was in his shirtsleeves with a fresh cup of coffee in his hand. "So, let's get into the details. Just to make sure we've covered everything."

Roslyn climbed up on a barstool. "Just like I said, I told him I was pregnant. At first he was all angry, grabbed at me—you know, what you'd expect. But as soon as he was convinced, he was happy. Said he'd take care of me."

George fingered his necktie. "So what does that mean? You ask him for money?"

"You could have knocked me over with a feather. I was expecting anger, fear, threats, and an offer of shut-up money, so I forget until after he left."

"Make-up sex?"

"He was on me like I was his last stop before a twenty-year prison stretch. But he wasn't rough. He was tender and"—she shrugged—"gentle. Called the baby his dream surprise." She laughed. "He's hoping for a son."

George shook his head. "He is one deluded bastard. So how do you want to work this? The original plan is out."

"I don't know."

George tapped his coffee cup on the counter. "You better think carefully because this looks like a one-way ticket. You see that, don't you? We bleed him for nine months. Then what? We run with the baby and you raise it, or we sell it to him and you never see it again. This is a hard, hard game. And how much trouble is his wife going to make?" He stacked their lunch plates and slid them down the counter toward the dishwasher. "There's no shame in saying you're not up for it. We've done all right here. We could pack up and leave. Make an appointment at a clinic in the next town."

"It's complicated. I'm kind of embarrassed to say this. I never wanted kids, but now, all of a sudden, it's like this is my last chance to be a mom."

"Listen to you. Forty-four years old and actually thinking about playing mommy. I told you that I'd back your play, and I'm not changing my mind. But what do you think life is going to be like if you keep the baby? You know how we live. Or do you think he's going to choose you over his rich wife? Put a ring on your finger and move you into the big house? What do you do then? Hang on long enough to earn a jackpot divorce settlement? How much of the money is even his?"

"I know I'm not making sense. Just give me a chance to work through my feelings. Next week is the first of April. There'll be ten grand in the PO box. We were going to stay here that long anyway."

George nodded. "Fair enough. Just keep me in the loop. You know how I hate surprises."

Billie sat in her Audi in the parking lot of the neighborhood park a few blocks from her house. The parking lot was well lit, and spotlights flooded the statute of Colonel Randal on horseback that was situated down the red brick walkway from the handicap ramp. The night was cooling rapidly and the wind was up. The forecast called for a 60 percent chance of light snow overnight, though the temperature was too warm for snow to stick. The sheriff pulled in beside her in his departmental cruiser, got out, and climbed into the passenger side of her car.

"Billie," he said, "I got your message. What's up with all the mystery? I could have driven over to your house."

"Donald thinks I went to the Pay-N-Pump to get some snacks."

"Okay. So you don't want him to know you're meeting me."

She put her hand on his shoulder. "The slut is knocked up."

He sighed. "I'm sorry for you, Billie, but I can't say that I'm surprised."

"Donald's talking like he wants to keep the baby. There's no time to wait for him to start making sense, so we've got to work around him."

"What have you got in mind?"

"Can you pick her up? Put her in a cell with some mean bitches? Trauma, stress—she gets in a bad fight. How do I know?"

The sheriff shook his head. "Billie, listen to yourself. I know you're stressed out, but really? Knowingly put a pregnant woman in danger? I could lose my office or end up in jail. I'm willing to help you, but that's a step too far. Besides, what makes you think he doesn't want a divorce or hasn't changed his mind about Congress?"

She told him what Donald had told her.

"He really has gone off the deep end. It wouldn't take ten minutes for a reporter to shatter the surrogate story."

"Exactly. You see what I'm up against."

He nodded. "And that's what got you going to crazy town."

"I'm sorry, Bo. I'm just at my wit's end."

"No need to apologize. Let's take a few days to think this through. I'm sure we can come up with something that makes sense."

The next morning, George sat in the living room, already dressed for work, and watched Roslyn putter about in the kitchen as she gathered together the elements of her healthy breakfast, a meal she'd religiously avoided the entire time he'd known her. This morning she seemed further lost in her maternal dreamscape, more convinced that somehow, beyond all hope, she could keep the baby and transform her life. Maybe it was a hormonal thing, something genetically designed to overcome logic and common sense to perpetuate the species. But maybe it wasn't. Maybe it was just some especially bad magical thinking. Maybe it was brought on by feeling that she was getting too old for the game, that he was going to dump her, that maybe she should take door number two while she still had a chance. And if that were the case, maybe she could be shocked out of it. It was dangerous, what with the sheriff and the PI breathing down their necks, but to keep Roslyn, it was worth the risk. "Hey, Roz, you remember that vacation house in the woods on the other side of the lake?"

She looked up from buttering her toast. "Yeah."

"It's been empty for weeks."

"I thought we were lying low, since the sheriff gave you a warning and that PI found us out."

"This is pretty safe. It's farther out. Less likely to be discovered. And rain is forecast for tomorrow, so if we catch it tonight, the rain will wash away the tracks."

"What about the PI?"

"We got the GPS tracker off the car. If he's following us, we cancel. If not, we get it done." He stood up. "Come on, it'll be fun. Get us out of the house. Give us something to do. God knows what we'll find in a place like that."

She smiled. "Okay."

That evening, under the heavy darkness from the thick cloud cover, they drove slowly down the potholed gravel access road that circled the far side of the lake. Two scraggly cedar trees framed the driveway they were looking for. The rusted metal mailbox, tilted out toward the road, held a week-old grocery store advertiser. They drove up the tree-lined driveway until they came to a fork in the road. It was left to the boat ramp, and right to the house. They parked off the driveway facing out. Through the near-leafless trees they could see the outline of the vacation house, a two-story rectangle with porches like a farmhouse. Lights were on in two of the upstairs windows. Roslyn put her hand on George's shoulder. "Are you sure this place is empty?"

"Absolutely. Owners won't be back from Arizona until May."

They crunched up the driveway on the loose gravel. Just as they entered the grassy yard on the kitchen side of the house, they heard a dog bark. They stopped in their tracks and listened. Another dog barked, farther away, and then another. They took three more steps before the kitchen light came on. As they turned in their tracks, a black and gray pit bull raced from around the corner of the house, barking and growling. "Christ," George said. "I'll decoy." They ran, the dog chasing. They heard yelling from back at the house. Roslyn ran straight down the driveway. George slowed and veered off to the right, looking for a tree he could climb, the pit bull gaining quickly. Gunshots rang out from behind them. George jumped for the limb of a maple tree, got his hands on it, and started to pull himself up. The pit bull leaped, snapped at George's ankle, landed on all fours, ran to pick up momentum, and leaped again, but George had scrambled over the limb. He stood on the heavy branch and leaned against the tree trunk to make himself invisible to anyone walking by on the ground. The dog trotted around the base of the tree, growling and wagging its tail. There was a whistle in the distance. The dog cocked his head. Another whistle. The dog disappeared. George counted slowly to ten. The woods were quiet. He dropped to the ground and jogged through the underbrush toward where he thought the Avalon was parked, moving slowly to avoid tripping in the dark. He hoped the shots had been random, and not aimed at Roslyn. When he came out of the woods at the fork in the driveway, the car was gone. He looked on both sides twice, as if he could have missed seeing it the first time, before he continued jogging down the driveway. The car was parked on the side of the access road with the engine running and the headlights off. He got in the passenger's side. "You okay, Roz? That was a close call."

She reached over and grabbed his hand. "Jesus, you scared me half to death."

George looked down the driveway. "Let's get out of here before they start after us."

She put the car in gear and pulled out onto the road. "My heart is still pounding."

He laughed. "You and me both. Did you see the jaws on the dog? Oh, my God. I thought I'd be riding a wheelchair for sure."

"You could have shot it."

"I was so busy running I forgot about my gun. Besides, I didn't need to hurt that dog."

"No more houses." She bumped through a deep pothole. "Christ. This is a moonscape." She turned on the headlights and increased her speed.

"You're right. No more houses. We've worn out our welcome on this little crime spree. We've run out of intelligence of where players are stashing their loot anyway. We got away clean, so we can call it good."

"You're acting like an adrenaline junky."

"Come on, be fair, how many times have I been this wrong on a job?"

"Once upon a time, somebody told me it only took one mistake one time to end up in prison for a long time."

"I'm glad you were paying attention."

She turned off of the gravel access road onto the county road blacktop.

Far behind them, driving without headlights, Jessup was following them in a beige Camry. He'd put a new tracker on the Avalon, up deep in the top of the driver's side front wheel well, so that it wouldn't be found after George found the decoy riding under the trunk just behind the back bumper. He knew where they had gone, and he'd been close enough to hear the gunshots. Initially, he'd planned to take a cut of this job just as he had the last time, but now he was glad he'd kept his distance. He didn't want to be part of any crime scene. When the GPS showed they were on the county road and gaining speed, he turned on his headlights. At the blacktop, he turned in the opposite direction.

Deputy Gruber pulled up to the farmhouse about thirty minutes later. All the downstairs lights were on. The Sanford family, who were housesitting for the Almires, was out in the yard. Mr. and Mrs. Sanford, in robes and pajamas, were cradling rifles. Mr. Sanford was a skinny, bald man with a long, gray mustache. Mrs. Sanford was just a bit taller than him. She wore gold-rimmed glasses. Her gray-blond hair hung loose around her shoulders. Their teenage son—in jeans, unlaced boots, and a flannel shirt, his hair dyed black and a red lightning bolt tattooed on his neck—held a black and gray pit bull on a chain leash. "You have a break-in?"

"Almost," Mr. Sanford said. "Freddy," he motioned with his head toward the dog, "got after them. Woke us up."

"I was in the kitchen, Dad," the teenager said.

"Get a look at them?" Deputy Gruber continued.

"A man and a woman, black clothes, black hats."

"We got them running," Mrs. Sanford said.

"I'm sure you did, ma'am. Could you make out any details?"

Mr. Sanford shook his head. "Too dark. They were in good shape, though. Ran fast. Heard their car, so they must have been parked somewhere down the driveway."

"When did you start house sitting here?"

"Ronnie Almire called us up last week. They'd been getting concerned about all the break-ins this winter. Thought their place was more isolated than most."

"Lucky call."

"Well, we'd been checking on the place all winter, but that's not the same as being here fulltime."

"Where do you live?"

"In town. Three-fifty-seven Maple Rock Avenue."

"I'll be back tomorrow morning to look for footprints, car tracks, or other evidence, so stay on the gravel if you need to leave."

"Okay," Mr. Sanford said.

"Have a good night."

8: Negotiations

A few days later, on the first of April, a sunny morning with new leaves budding on the trees, Roslyn and Honeycutt sat in Honeycutt's Cadillac in the parking lot of the KFC on Simmons Boulevard, across the street from Security Shipping. Honeycutt had dropped off the mailer containing $10,000 promptly at 7:30 a.m., just as the sheriff had instructed, and since he wanted to meet Roslyn before he went to the bank, and the KFC parking lot was busy in the early morning, this seems the likely spot. A chicken biscuit wrapper and an empty milk carton lay on the console between them. "So this is how it is," Honeycutt said. "I want the baby. If you don't want the baby, I do. If you want the baby, then I want joint custody."

"Joint custody? So you're going to be with me?"

"I won't divorce Billie. I love her. What I will do is sign legal papers giving you alimony for life if you give me joint custody."

"I'm not going to be your baby momma or your mistress. If you want this baby, then you have to choose me."

"You need to think this through. I'm talking about what's best for the baby. You're not going to get a better or fairer offer."

"I have thought this through. I have the baby. You want the baby. So right now I have the leverage. I could leave tomorrow."

"With no money? I'd track you down and take you to court."

"The publicity would ruin your marriage. No, Donny, eventually you're going to have to choose your dream — family man or congressman. So you might as well choose now."

"You can't take my son away."

"Your son? How about my daughter? Until I take a paternity test, you don't have a baby. And you can't make me take the test."

"Think it over, Roz. You need to come up with the magic number that's going to leave you feeling good about moving on."

"Moving on? Donald, I want our baby to grow up with you. I want to build our lives together. But I won't be bullied. You decide what you want to do. Just don't take too long." She pecked him on the cheek and got out of the Cadillac.

He watched her get into her Lincoln and drive away. He folded up the chicken biscuit wrapper and pushed it into the empty milk carton. Why were women so demanding? He knew what Billie wanted—an abortion and a pay-off followed by a successful election—and now he knew what Roslyn wanted. With Billie, the problem was getting her to accept the baby. The baby wasn't hers. The baby represented his infidelities. But Billie had a big heart, so she could, with time, learn to love the baby. Particularly if he kept his promise to change his ways and be true to her. With Roslyn, the problem was getting her to give him the baby. Right now, she was right. She did have the upper hand. She could ruin his and Billie's plans. Even if Roslyn exposed his infidelity to the press, he'd still want the baby. And she knew it. But if Billie's dreams were shattered, she'd always blame the baby. That was the quandary. So he had to win the election, which meant that he had to convince Roslyn to give him the baby. How was he going to do that? He had to win her trust, just like he had to win Billie's. He was sure that he could keep Billie and the baby if he could get both Billie and Roslyn to trust him. The only leverage he currently had was that they both needed him to achieve their dreams. Billie wanted to go to Washington and Roslyn wanted to be a mom. He started his car. How could he use that knowledge to his advantage?

Midmorning, Sheriff Teardale was parked at the KFC in his departmental cruiser when George came out of Security Shipping with Donald's mailer tucked under his arm. The sheriff had to shake his head at the brazenness of it. Cody Yu had made sure that Kenny, the employee who rented the black-mailer his mailbox, was working today. And Kenny had called with a description when he saw George walking in the front door. Traffic was light. The sheriff let George drive away, following him east on Simmons Boulevard and waiting until he turned right on Maple Street into a quiet residential neighbor-hood before he pulled him over. He didn't want witnesses. He put on his sheriff's department cap before he walked back to George's Cadillac. "Good morning, Mr. Harrison. Please get out of the car."

"What's this about?"

"Please get out of the car."

George got out. The sheriff towered over him, his heavy shoulders straining the fabric of his shirt, his big hand on the butt of his holstered pistol.

"Place both hands on the hood."

"There must be some mistake."

"Both hands on the hood."

George stepped to the side of the car and put his hands on the hood.

The sheriff came up behind him, kicked George's feet farther apart, grabbed his right wrist, cuffed it, and then grabbed the left and cuffed his wrists together behind his back. "You're under arrest."

"Arrest? What for?"

"Blackmail."

The sheriff shoved George into the backseat of the cruiser, knocking him against the doorjamb in the process, and then went back to the Cadillac, picked up the mailer, locked the car, and put the keys in his pocket. As he walked back to his cruiser, he looked into the open mailer. It was full of money. He tossed the mailer into the passenger seat as he sat down behind the wheel.

"I don't have any idea what's in that envelope," George said.

"Uh-huh."

"Matter of fact, I've never seen it before. It certainly wasn't in my car."

"Uh-huh."

"So I wouldn't miss it if I never saw it again."

The sheriff looked over his shoulder. "You think I would steal from my own family? Shut up." He put the cruiser in gear, and said into the windshield, "We'll send a wrecker for your vehicle."

When they got to the county jail, the sheriff pulled up at the back next to a half-filled, rust-red Dumpster and used a key to open an unmarked gray steel door. Then he escorted George down a freshly painted, cream-white concrete block hallway and into an interrogation room, where he cuffed him to a steel ring set into a gray metal desk that was bolted to the floor. No one seemed to be in this part of the jail. "Have a seat. You want a soda, cup of coffee or something?"

"I want a lawyer."

"We'll get to that."

The sheriff left the room. George looked up at the video camera hanging from the ceiling in the corner behind the door. It was unplugged. The room was warm, and there didn't seem to be any air circulation. George had been in rooms like this before. Worst case he'd be smacked around and threatened. But this wasn't the movies. The cops would eventually get frustrated and bored. He'd get his lawyer. They had $10,000 in an envelope. That money wasn't evidence of a crime unless Honeycutt made it evidence. And Honeycutt wasn't going to do that.

After a while, the sheriff came back. His gun holster was empty. "How do you like this room? It's part of the new addition. Still under construction. Air handlers aren't online yet."

"I'd like a lawyer, please."

The sheriff pulled his baton, stepped around the table, and gave George a two-handed jab in the stomach, knocking the air out of him. When he jerked forward, the sheriff kicked the chair out from under him. He fell to the floor, his hands cuffed to the steel ring above his head. The sheriff gave him a hard kick in the ribs, whacked his cuffed hands with the baton, kicked him in the kidney, and whacked his shoulder with the baton. "Have I got your attention? The last time we spoke, I don't believe I had your attention."

George felt the vomit rise in his throat but swallowed it down.

The sheriff looked at him with lizard eyes. "You were trying to blackmail my sister-in-law. I told you to get out of town. For your own safety." He kicked him in the groin. "But you don't seem much interested in your safety. Is that right?"

"I am."

"I am what?"

"I am interested in my own safety."

"Really? I'm surprised. I was beginning to believe it was going to be the lake, the landfill or the car crusher for you. And your wife."

"We can go. We can leave today. This minute."

"You scammed my sister-in-law's retarded husband. Got your wife knocked up. That doesn't sound like someone in a hurry to leave."

"The pregnancy was an accident."

The sheriff bent over him and punched him in the face. "Is that right?"

Blood ran from George's nose. "That's right."

"I want the February and March money back."

"I'll get it."

"I know you will." He righted the chair, pulled George up by the shoulder, and slid the chair back under him. "Looks like you're going to have two black eyes. Is that a problem for you?"

"No, sir."

"I believe we really are talking to each other now. What's your plans?"

"We're leaving town."

"Wonderful. Because I'm going to be very angry with you if you make me kill a pregnant woman. And that could affect whether you go into the car crusher alive or dead."

The sheriff uncuffed him from the table. "Can you walk?"

"Yes, sir."

"Good. Let's take you to the hospital. That was a hell of a car wreck. You were lucky to get out of there alive."

The sheriff half dragged George by the arm back down the hall and out into the parking lot. George blinked in the glare. Two sheriff's department SUVs were now parked next to the sheriff's cruiser, but there was still no one in sight. A swarm of flies were buzzing around the Dumpster. The sheriff shoved George into the back seat of the cruiser. George lay down on his side. When they arrived at the Tri-County Medical Center, the sheriff pulled up to the doors at the emergency entrance in the circle drive, opened the back door to the cruiser, and helped George out. George stood hunched over with his arms wrapped around his middle. The sheriff tossed George's car keys at him. "Get patched up and get the hell out of here." He watched as George bent down to pick up his keys off the pavement and then stumbled toward the automatic doors of the emergency entrance.

The sheriff sat down in his car, mopped his brow, and got out his cell phone. "Billie. I think I just solved all your problems. George Harrison was the ten-thousand-dollar blackmailer."

"Really?

"Watched him leave the mailbox with the envelope."

"Maybe my luck is finally changing. How did you leave it?"

"I just dropped him at the emergency room. They're leaving town as soon as he's seen to. And I'm getting your money back."

"They won't give us any more trouble?"

"I made a believer out of him."

"Thanks, Bo."

"I'm not against a little street justice, Billie, but I've gone as far over the line as I'm willing to go, so I hope for your sake that this is all of it."

"Me too."

Roslyn came through the automatic doors into the reception area of the emergency department of the Tri-County Medical Center. An overweight couple dressed in faded, baggy clothes sat in chairs with a good view of the TV. Roslyn went up to the counter. The nurse looked up from her computer screen. "I got a call that George Harrison was here."

The nurse's expression turned quizzical.

"I'm his wife."

She nodded. "Follow me."

She led her back through the double doors on the left side of the counter. George was lying in a screened-off bed in one of the bays. His eyes were black, his nose had been more or less straightened and packed, and his ribs were taped. The blood had been washed off of him, although there were still traces in the creases of his neck. Roslyn stood over him, shaking her head. "How do you feel?"

"I've felt better." He tried to smile. "Looks worse than it is."

She moved to hold his hand, saw the bruises and changed her mind. She leaned down and whispered, "Who did this?"

"Sheriff. Caught me with the envelope. We have to give the money back and get out of town."

"Or?"

"Short, painful trip to a shallow grave."

"Donald didn't know about this."

"Don't try your luck, sweetie. I'm not moving very fast right now."

"I'll be right back." Roslyn walked through the double doors to the reception area and out into the parking lot. She called Honeycutt. "I'm in the middle of something," he said. "Can I call you back?"

"No. I'm at the emergency room."

"Emergency room? Are you okay?"

She leaned against her car. "Your brother-in-law beat up George. So I guess this is good-bye."

"What? What are you talking about? Just calm down."

"Calm down? George is all busted up. They're going to kill us if we don't get out of town." She hung up. She looked off across the street at the Pay-N-Pump on the corner. A young mother and her grade-school daughter wearing matching leather jackets were walking across the parking lot with soda cups in their hands. Her phone rang. It was Honeycutt.

"Okay, Roslyn, don't hang up. Bo beat up George?"

"Threatened to kill us if we didn't disappear."

"That's just bluster. He's not that kind of a guy."

"That's what you say."

"I'll take care of this. You've got nothing to worry about. Are they keeping George in the hospital?"

"I don't know."

"Just relax. I'm going to fix this right now." He hung up.

Roslyn watched the mother and daughter get into a metallic blue minivan. The sun was warm. She wasn't there yet, but she was beginning to get the feeling that she could get Donald wrapped around her finger. He was already used to being told what to do. It was just going to take a while for him to get used to her doing the telling. She went back into the emergency department. George looked at her expectantly. "Donald is going to take care of it."

"You really think he has any pull with the sheriff?"

She shrugged. "As long as Billie needs him, we're going to be okay."

Honeycutt closed the door to his office, sat on the corner of his desk and dialed the sheriff's number. "Bo? Got a minute?"

"I thought you might be calling."

"Lay off the Harrisons."

"They were the ones blackmailing you for ten thousand a month."

"What? Come on—"

"I followed Harrison myself. There's no doubt. He went to the mailbox. I've got the envelope with your money in it."

Honeycutt bit his lip. "I still want them left alone."

"You're insane. You know that, don't you?"

"I don't have to explain myself to you."

"And I don't work for you. Call your wife; it's up to her." He hung up.

Honeycutt picked up the picture of Billie that sat on the corner of his desk and looked at it. Billie was standing beside a pockmarked boulder at the beach. She was wearing an African print spaghetti-strap cover-up. The wind was in her hair and her smile lit up her face. When had he taken that picture? The third year of their marriage? He smiled to himself. Florida in February. The weather had been gorgeous. That was the year he got her to go skydiving. He set the picture back down. How had they gotten from there to here? That Billie would have done anything he wanted. The only chance he had of convincing her now was to talk with her in person. He picked up his phone and called her.

"Donny, what's up?"

"Where are you?"

"I'm in my office at home."

"I'm coming over. I need to see you right away."

"What about?"

He hung up before she could get to "no." Driving across town, all he could think about was how important it was to get Billie on to his side. The pieces of the puzzle would all fit together if Billie would let them. They could win the election, go to Washington, and keep the baby. It was all doable. If she would just accept the baby and quit antagonizing Roslyn, Roslyn would settle down and he could massage her into seeing that she needed to give up his son and move on. It was, after all, in her best interest. He just had to keep working on influencing her decision making, and he couldn't do that if she was scared. If she were scared, she was going to cling to her husband, and his bad advice made everything a lot more complicated than it needed to be. He was a liability. But at least he responded to money. Maybe there was a way to use him to get Roslyn to leave the baby and go. Honeycutt turned into his driveway. He couldn't be that lucky. They would be better off if Roslyn and her husband had a falling out. With him out of the picture, Honeycutt knew he could get Roslyn to do what he wanted.

Honeycutt came in from the garage to the kitchen. The house was quiet. "Billie," he hollered.

"In here."

He walked back through the front hall to the living room. Billie was standing at the window by the fireplace. She turned and looked at him. "So what's this all about?"

Honeycutt shut the door. "You know what this is about."

"You look like you could use a drink. I'm going to have one. You want one?" She walked over to the drinks cabinet.

"I don't want a drink. Roslyn phoned me from the hospital. Bo worked over Harrison, threatened to kill them."

Billie poured herself a short glass of red wine from a previously opened bottle sitting out on top of the cabinet. "That sounds like an exaggeration."

"You're going to tell Bo to leave them alone."

"Donny, they're criminals. They extorted thirty thousand from us. They tried to extort another sixty thousand. They belong in prison. They're lucky to be run out of town."

"I don't care what they did. She's carrying my baby."

"And you don't care about how that might have happened? That it was just part of a plan to rob us?"

"That doesn't change the one fact that matters. I'm a father. And if you want to go to Washington, you're going to make sure nothing happens to the baby momma."

"Donny, think about what you're saying. They extort us, and you give me ultimatums. Just think about how crazy that sounds."

"I don't care how crazy it sounds."

She pushed the glass of wine into his hand and poured herself another. "And you don't care that they might just be using the baby as leverage to steal from us."

"Don't care."

She nodded. "Okay. What are we going to do about them after the baby is born?"

"I'm open to suggestion."

"Open to suggestion? You really mean that?"

"I really mean it."

"No setting her up in a house or putting her on an allowance or any other nonsense just as long as you keep the baby?"

"We keep the baby; you can do whatever you think is best."

"And if I call off Bo, you'll quit pissing around and focus your attention on winning the race?"

"You have my word."

She sat on the sofa and patted the seat next to her. "Sit down." He sat. "I've done a little research. For right now, we'll operate as if the baby is yours. Tomorrow, Roslyn has that appointment with Natalie that we already set up. We'll make sure Roslyn's health is good. At fourteen weeks, we can do the amniocentesis to get the paternity and disability tests. If the baby really is yours, I'll do everything I can to help you get custody. Is that fair?"

Honeycutt nodded.

"In the meantime, we need to plan our cover up. If this affair and the baby get out, we're wrecked. The campaign will be over. I understand how important this baby is to you. I really do. But you know how it is with me. I don't care if you fool around, but I won't put up with anything serious. We have plans. You're my husband. You need to come back to my bed where you belong."

Honeycutt drank off his wine. "I don't know why, but I'm going to be honest with you. I don't trust you. You don't want my baby. You see my baby as a problem that you'd like solved, sooner rather than later. And until I see some change in you, I'm going to be on my guard."

"So you cheated on me, put all our plans at risk, and I have to prove myself to you? Is that how you see it?"

"That's not what I said."

"Then what did you say?"

"I screwed up, okay? I put myself in a situation where we could be taken advantage of. I regret that. I want to make that right. I didn't plan on the baby. I didn't try for the baby. But I won't give up my baby. Moving forward, any plan that includes me includes my son."

"Your son? How do you know it's a boy?"

"I don't, okay? I just have this feeling. Not that it matters. Any plan that includes me includes my baby."

"Fair enough." Billie picked up the phone on the end table by the window. Outside, she could see the neighbor's black lab chasing the birds from under their backyard bird feeder. "Bo? How are you? Change of plan. Leave the Harrisons alone. We'll handle it."

The sheriff hung up the phone. He hoped she had made a good decision, but he was glad to be out of it. There were one hundred ways to screw things up and only a few ways to fix them. He turned his attention to the crime numbers in the report on his desk and compared them with last year's numbers in the report on his laptop. Drunk driving, robbery, domestic violence—everything was in the usual ranges except for breaking and entering, where there were too many unsolved cases.

Deputy Gruber knocked on the sheriff's open door. "Got a minute?"

The sheriff took off his black-framed glasses as he looked up. The deputy was wearing cowboy boots, jeans, and a flannel shirt. "Marvin, come on in. Why you down here on your day off?"

The deputy sat down in one of the visitor's chairs. "Remember that attempted robbery on the other side of the lake a few nights ago?"

"Yeah. The Almires' fishing place."

"I think it might be related to the break-in out at Lakeview Estates last week."

"Jimmy and Faith's?"

The deputy nodded.

"That was just a broken garage window. They report anything missing?"

"No."

"So what makes you think it was a break-in?"

"If it was an accident, where was the rock or the ball or whatever broke the window? The garage was empty, except for the broken glass."

"How's it like the Almires'?"

"Tire tracks in the clay down at the bottom of the drive look like the tracks out at the Almires'. I took casts."

The sheriff nodded thoughtfully. "So you think we might have a break-in crew targeting empty houses. Mighty thin, Marvin."

The deputy leaned forward with his elbows on his knees. "There was that break-in back in January out at Riverview Heights. No leads there, either."

"Thought that was vandalism."

The deputy shrugged. "Looked like vandalism."

"Well, we don't have any other leads, so you might as well get the state guy to analyze the casts. See where it goes."

"Thanks, boss."

Honeycutt drove back to the bank. Sunlight dappled through the new leaves on the trees lining the street in front of the elementary school at the corner with Pilot Road. It was recess. Children ran and hollered across the schoolyard, kicking balls, playing tag, jumping onto the monkey bars. He called Roslyn from his cell phone. "It's all taken care of. You have nothing to be afraid of. The sheriff won't bother you anymore."

"Are you sure?"

"Positive. Just stay out of trouble. Keep a low profile and everything will be fine."

"Thank you, Donald. I really appreciate it."

"And you know how to show your appreciation."

"I do."

"See you tomorrow for the doctor's appointment."

"I can't wait."

Honeycutt hung up. The traffic light at the intersection had just turned red. He slowed to a stop. The sheriff's meddling had ironically worked to his advantage, giving him the opportunity to make progress with both Billie and Roslyn. He'd gotten Billie to approve, at least on the surface, his plan to keep his son, and he'd shown Roslyn that he had the power to do what he said he would do. George Harrison in the emergency room was just a bonus. The traffic light turned green. He waited for the on-coming cars and took a left turn.

Later that evening, Honeycutt and Billie sat in a booth at Freddy's Drive Away, a diner with gas pumps at the inter-section of Highway 12 and Q Street in Pender County, across the street from an abandoned drive-in movie theater and catty-cornered to a grain elevator. Most of the stools at the counter were occupied, and most the booths were full. Pender County Sheriff Michaels and Pender County Chair of the County Commission Withers sat across from them. They were all drinking coffee. Their just-finished dinner plates were still on the table in front of them. Commissioner Withers, a local insurance agent, wore a blue blazer, white shirt and red and blue striped tie. Sheriff Michaels wore jeans and a flannel shirt with a sheriff's department cap. A fringe of white hair stuck out between his ears and the edge of the cap. He held his coffee cup in both hands. "My reelection fund is just fine. Nobody's running against me."

Withers smiled. "Nobody would be foolish enough to waste the time or money."

Honeycutt nodded. "Lucky man. But you've got meth here just like everywhere."

The sheriff shrugged.

"We'll grease the drug task force money for you. We know Representative Daniels doesn't like you. That he's been dragging his feet."

"That's all a silly misunderstanding. I never called him that name. That was just Bill Dobbs fishing for campaign help."

"Yeah, but a black man can be touchy about the 'N' word. Bottom line, you support us, and we'll remember it in January. And we've got to run every two years, so we're not going to forget."

Their waitress set their check in the middle of the table and picked up their plates.

"More coffee?"

They all shook their heads. She walked away.

"So," Billie said, "can we count on your help?"

The sheriff and Withers glanced at each other. "We'd prefer to work with you," Withers said, "but here in Pender County we all like to row together. So let us talk with the other county commissioners and we'll get back to you."

They all stood and shook hands. Billie picked up the check. She and Honeycutt stopped at the cash register to pay. The sheriff and the commissioner walked around the side of the diner to where they had parked their cars. The waitress came up to the cash register and rang up the bill. "How was everything?"

"Everything was great," Billie said. "Just great."

George, dressed in blue flannel pajamas, was sitting in the living room playing free cell on his laptop when his phone rang. His nose was taped, but his eyes were more purplish than black. He held one arm over his taped ribs while he reached for the phone on the coffee table with his other hand. "Hello?"

"Mr. Harrison. This is your new best friend, Stan Jessup. We met last week out at Lakeview Estates."

There was traffic noise on the line, as if Jessup were standing outside somewhere. "Why are we speaking?" George asked.

"The cops are looking hard at the attempted robbery out at the farmhouse across the lake."

"So?"

"I know you were out there."

George chuckled. "Nice try."

"You didn't find the GPS tracker up in the front left wheel well, did you? You want me to tell you where you were at what time?"

"What do you want?"

"I'm not greedy. Two thousand should do it."

"It was an attempted robbery."

"Don't care. I still need two grand to keep quiet."

"Why don't I just kill you?"

"Kill me? Be serious. You're making too much money off the Honeycutts to leave just yet. I'm just looking for a taste."

"Give me a call tomorrow."

"Now you're talking. Take care."

George sat back on the sofa. This job had developed way too many complications, some of which he'd brought on himself. They had Jessup on their backs because they had decided to go after that safe. Thought they would be leaving town and it wouldn't matter, but you can't predict the future. You have to be prepared. That was on him. He misinterpreted the sheriff's possible involvement when he tried for the extra $60,000, which probably put them under increased scrutiny. That was on him as well. But if Roz hadn't gotten pregnant and gone off script, he wouldn't have suggested the Almires' cabin as a way to get her back on track. Didn't work, but he had to try. And Honeycutt gave up the PO box. That was the only way the sheriff could have found out. That had to have happened after the pregnancy, but it wasn't anybody's fault. Just plain bad luck. And now this latest Jessup bullshit. He shifted his weight on the sofa and a sharp pain shot through the ribs on his right side. He was in no condition to fight it out. They needed to take their winnings and get out of town. But Roz wouldn't leave as long as she thought she was making progress with Honeycutt, and he couldn't leave Roz. There had to be some way to make her see reason.

Honeycutt and Billie drove home from Pender County in silence; Honeycutt behind the wheel of the Cadillac, Billie in the passenger's seat, the talk radio turned down so low that it was really just an excuse not to speak. The night was cloudy, with light fog in the low areas, which made the driving more difficult on the dark county roads and made the city streets seem brighter under the streetlights. Billie sat turned away from him looking out her side window. She felt empty and lonely. She was tired of assessing blame, tired of feeling the tension between her and Donald, tired of pretending for strangers. After they pulled into their garage and the garage door started to come down, Billie turned in her seat to look at him. "Before we go into the house, I've got something that I want to say."

"Okay."

"We've always been good together. Just like tonight at the diner. We sold them and now they'll sell their friends."

He nodded.

"I know I got off on the wrong foot about the baby. I was jealous. I admit it. I guess I have unresolved feelings about being infertile. But I want you to be happy. I do. But you can understand how this hurt me, can't you? Especially right now. We're partners. We have commitments to each other. I want to make up. I want things to be right between us. If the paternity checks out, I'll do everything I can to open my heart to that baby."

Honeycutt took her hands in his. "I love you, Billie. I never wanted any trouble between us."

"Will you make up with me?"

"I never wanted us to be apart."

"You really mean that?"

"Yes."

She leaned over and kissed him. "Then prove it." She shoved the passenger's door open and ran out of the garage, leaving the door to the kitchen open. He smiled. It was a familiar game. He came after her, swung the door to the kitchen closed, kicked off his shoes, charged up the stairs two steps at a time in the wake of her high heels, skirt and blouse, and tackled her in the bedroom. They rolled on the carpet. He hoisted her on his shoulder as she kicked and play fought, then slammed the bedroom door shut with his foot. He staggered. She wriggled free, ran around to the other side of the bed, stood there catching her breath as she unhooked her bra and slinked out of her panties. He shrugged off his suit coat and shirt, kicked his pants off, and dove over the bed after her. She ran around to the other side of the bed, laughing as she went. He rolled over on the bed, pulled off his socks and boxers, and sprang up after her. She ran toward her bathroom, but he caught her up, wriggling, pulled her tight, and kissed her lips. She wrapped her legs around his waist and her arms around his neck. He crab-walked to the bed, tossed her down, and flipped her onto her belly. He'd never noticed before how much she looked like Roslyn. A little rounder, a little softer. He grabbed her shoulders and pulled himself up inside her. She gasped. They each started moving and they fell into rhythm. He smiled, his eyes half-closed. The sex had always been good. He didn't know why, but he still didn't believe her, still didn't believe that she would accept his son, even now, after she'd given herself to him. Maybe she was just selling it too hard. He reached up and grabbed a handful of her hair. He thought of Roslyn, of his baby, of being a father. "I love you," he said.

She smiled, her face in the sheet. "I love you."

9: The Best Laid Plans

The next morning, Honeycutt and Roslyn drove around to the back of the Women's Health Clinic, which was sandwiched between Yusef Podiatry and She Spirit Yoga across the street from the Tri-County Medical Center. The Women's Health Clinic was a solo practice operated by Dr. Natalie Binder, OB/GYN, who was Billie's second cousin. Honeycutt parked the Cadillac in an "employee only" parking space and pressed the buzzer at the back door. Dr. Binder's nurse, Iris, a slim, middle-aged woman with curly gray hair cut short around her head, ushered Honeycutt and Roslyn into the hallway. Dr. Binder stepped out of an examination room into the hall. She wore black pants, black lace-up walking shoes and a white coat over a button-down pink Oxford cloth shirt. A thin gold chain hung around her neck and her shoulder-length light brown hair was held back out of her face by two gold barrettes. A short scar was visible on her left cheek. "Donald. There you are. How's Billie?"

"She's fine."

She turned to Roslyn. "You must be Joan." They shook hands. She turned to her nurse. "Iris, put Joan in room three. And put Mr. Honeycutt in my office."

Dr. Binder's office was in the back corner of the clinic. A glass-topped desk with a computer on it sat to the left, two office chairs facing it. An overstuffed reading chair sat under the window. Honeycutt sat in the reading chair, got out his smartphone, and started reading the online version of the *Randal Junction Gazette*. About an hour later, Dr. Binder came into the office, turned the nearest office chair toward him, and sat down. "I don't have to tell you what I'd do if my husband were in the situation that you're in."

"Fortunately, you're not my wife."

"Well, at least that's something we can agree on. Your friend is pregnant. Very early. Her health is fine. We're doing all the usual blood work, plus an STD screen. Took a urine sample. You can check the results online in the next few days. I gave her some advice about morning sickness, etc., which doesn't concern you. As I told Billie, we'll charge this out to her account, but we won't run insurance on it, so it's all out of pocket. I gave her my number in case she has any medical questions or any problems arise."

"Problems?"

"I don't expect anything. Being pregnant is normal. She's just a bit old. She's got her next appointment scheduled. She should come through the front door with her husband — that conversation is going to be a doozy — or by herself."

"When can we find out the sex?"

"Ultrasound after sixteen weeks. So it will be a while."

"Thanks, Natalie."

She stood up. "Don't thank me, you bastard. I wouldn't be in the same room with you if it weren't a personal favor to my cousin. Let's go collect the lucky lady."

Honeycutt backed out of his parking space and started back around the building. The sun was in his eyes. He squinted and pushed down the sun visor. "Binder told me that everything was fine."

"Yeah," Roslyn said, "she's really nice. I don't think I've ever been to a doctor who had such a gentle touch."

Honeycutt drove down to the Pump-N-Pay on the corner, turned in, and parked away from the building. In his rearview mirror, he could see three cars at the pumps. A woman dressed for the office, her red suit coat hanging open, was walking between the pumps and the store. Honeycutt turned to Roslyn. His hands were tingling. He knew he was about to do something really crazy, but it was simply a matter of winning her trust. "I've been thinking about our situation."

"Have you got a new offer?"

"I think maybe we should get married before the baby is born."

"Really? Married? When are you going to tell Billie?"

"So you would marry me?"

She looked at his face as if she could see straight through him. "A real marriage? Not just some bullshit convenience."

He nodded.

"Yeah, I'd marry you."

He smiled a wacky, cartoon smile. "Good. I mean, great. This is the best news I've gotten since the baby."

She kept watching him. "So how does this work?"

"We've got to be very careful. We've got to go slow. For Billie to get her mind around this, we have to go step by step. First we get to the point where there can't be an abortion."

"I'm not getting an abortion."

"I know. But Billie is going to hold out hope until it's too late, because it's the option that makes her life the simplest. Then we get through the primary. Somewhere between June and November, the time will be right. Maybe we'll get divorced after the election. I don't know. We'll just have to feel along. You and George are safe. We've got nine months, more or less."

"You're serious?"

He nodded.

"Okay, I get what you're saying. Only, how am I going to live? And pay my bills? George is going to want to be paid."

"I'll just keep on paying the ten thousand. Only now we don't need the drop box. How about that? I'll just give the money to you."

"Okay."

"So what are you going to do about George? You could divorce him anytime. Are you really married?"

"Yeah, you're right. I could divorce him anytime. But right now he takes care of me, runs errands, keeps me company. And he's the cover story for me being pregnant. But don't worry," she snapped her fingers, "when it's time I'll get rid of him just like that."

"Okay. But I don't want you sleeping with him anymore. You're mine now. I'm paying the freight. You belong to me."

112

"Okay, Donny."

"I'm not kidding."

"I know you're not kidding." She reached over, put her hand on his crotch, and kissed him affectionately.

He looked in the rearview mirror again. The gas pumps were empty. "Are you in a hurry?"

She smiled. "What have you got in mind?"

"I know about a little drive-in spot in the city park that will be well hidden now that the leaves are coming back out."

"Let's have a look."

That afternoon, lying in bed in their apartment with the blinds half-drawn, Roslyn told George the details of her morning escapades. "Seriously? That's his plan?" George held his arm around his ribs to keep them from hurting while he laughed.

Roslyn sat up against the oak headboard and pulled the sheet up to cover her breasts. "God's honor."

"At least we get to keep the money." George chuckled. "I just don't understand how that guy could be smart enough to be a bank executive. Unless," George turned his head and looked up at her, "he's crazy like a fox. No matter what you or Billie say, once abortion is off the table, he's got more leverage. Let's say it's October. The baby's due. He says no hard feelings but I'm not marrying you. And by the way, I'll only give you money if you give me the baby. What do you do then?"

"Nuclear option. I wreck his chances of becoming congressman and ruin his marriage."

"And once you go to the press, he loses the race and his wife, maybe, but he can go to court, have you declared an unfit mother and take the baby. Or, let's say you blink, he wins. He can drop you whenever he wants because the worst you can do won't move him." He sat up next to her. "Does that make sense? Your only solid angles are abortion or running off with the baby. Because the only thing we know for sure is that he wants the baby, which means his leverage increases every step of the way.

She nodded. "And to run off with the baby, I have to want the baby more than sharing the baby for whatever scraps he'll give me."

113

"Bingo. So what are you going to do right now?"

"I've still got time to figure out his hand. I'm going to act like I'm going along. Quit pretending I'm a real estate agent. Sign up for an exercise class. You can quit, too, if you want."

George shook his head. "As soon as the tape come off my nose, I'm going back to work. Need to keep busy and give our buddy Stan something to do."

"Georgie." She patted his leg. "Are we going to pay him?"

"Can't kill him and stay in town, no matter how deep we bury him, so he's got us over a barrel until we're ready to leave. He is going to pull that GPS tracker, though. And I'm going to make sure he doesn't set another one."

"I'm sorry I'm being so indecisive. I know you like to be action man."

"Just want to stay one step ahead of trouble."

"I'm going to shower."

George watched her disappear into the bathroom, her bare ass jiggling ever so slightly as she walked. Her thinking was still becoming more magical day by day. And she hadn't mentioned the most obvious fallout of her choices. If she could actually get Honeycutt to marry her, then George was out of the picture. If she chose to stay in town and play baby momma, then he was also out of her plan. There were only two ways that they could stay together. One, if they took a payoff from Billie to avoid the scandal and Roslyn had an abortion, or if they got what money they could and Roslyn left with him and kept the baby— however that crazy situation would work out. He'd have to plan a retirement scam, bring in three or four friends, knock over something big and dangerous. They couldn't travel and scam with a grade school kid in tow. Too many questions. Maybe he should just walk away. Find a woman about ten years younger than Roslyn. Train her up. Could that possibly work? He could hear the shower running. No. Roz was his girl. He could read her while he was working a mark, and, more importantly, she could read him. They were completely in tune from years of experience. They knew each other, but nobody knew them. He'd be crippled without her. Besides, he was in love with her. He couldn't imagine life without her. He had to find a way to wake her up, get her back on course, reel her in.

There was still good money to be made here if he could get her back on her toes. He had to find a way.

Billie sat in Evelyn's office at the campaign headquarters. A multicolored silk scarf was wrapped around her throat, covering a long scratch that Donald had accidentally given her last night. The door to the office was closed, but they could still hear the phones and printers from the front room through the large window in the wall. Billie had been thinking about this conversation all morning, thinking about it, really, since she woke in the night with Donald snoring beside her, but she wasn't really sure yet if she knew the right words. "Let me give you the good news first," she said. "Dean Withers called after lunch. The Pender County officials are on board with us. Not surprising, but it's still good to check them off."

Evelyn leaned forward, her reading glasses swinging from the chain around her neck. "You and Donald are unstoppable when it comes to closing a deal."

"Thank you." Billie smiled. "So that leaves the suburban mayors."

Billie sipped her coffee. Evelyn looked across her desk expectantly. "The bad news?"

"Donald is becoming way too close with Roslyn Harrison. He's losing perspective. I can't seem to get him back on course."

"You told me that you could handle this."

"Believe me, if he'd been wearing a leash, his neck would be raw."

"Why are you telling me? This isn't my area."

"We need to find someone new."

"We? He's your husband. Can't you keep him occupied?"

"I wish it were that easy. I pulled all the stops last night, but I'm just not convinced I can trust him. It's humiliating, but that's the way it is."

"What about someone at the bank?"

"No one there is foolish enough to face the fallout."

Evelyn looked out of the window of her office into the front room. Three young women, two brunettes and one blonde, sat at desks working at computers. "I can't do it."

"Evelyn, everyone has to earn their pay. Donald's infatuated. If he keeps on, I'm going to lose a husband, and you're going to lose a candidate. We're going to win if we can just drag his sorry ass across the finish line. I know it; you know it. Hell, even the interns know it. I'll be able to whip him into shape once we're in Washington. Right? Out of sight, out of mind. Work with me here. You win this race. We give you glowing reviews. You'll have your pick of candidates in the next election. You'll have to hire someone to count your money."

"I won't pimp."

"You think I want more people screwing my husband? Distraction. That's what we need."

"Okay. I'll see what I can do."

Billie left the office. Evelyn shuffled the papers on her desk together and put them into a file folder. She looked through her window at the young women at their desks. Robyn—dark hair, glasses, navy turtleneck—was too serious. She'd quit, stomp out of here, and go online. Gail—dark hair, no makeup, pixie tattoo on her shoulder—all her friends seemed to be women. She just might start laughing out loud at the suggestion. But Sherri—blond, bubbly personality, always wearing shirts with one too many buttons unbuttoned—Evelyn shook her head. Why did she always stereotype women who looked like that? Was Sherri sophisticated enough to maintain a "hands off the candy" policy? Evelyn put the file folder into the desk file drawer. She should have quit when Billie first brought her the news of the affair. But Billie was right. As long as no one found out about the baby momma, Donald was going to be the next congressman. Evelyn would count her win and move on. If the house of cards fell on them afterward, they had no one to blame but themselves. She just needed to make sure there was nothing she did that she could be blamed for. She got up and went to the door. "Sherri," she yelled, "could you come here, please?"

Evelyn was sitting behind her desk when Sherri came to the door. Her white blouse was unbuttoned to expose her lacy pink bra. Her skinny jeans were tucked into cowgirl boots and accented with a matching belt sporting a big silver buckle. She held a pad in one hand and a pencil in the other. "What's up, Ev?"

Evelyn smiled. "I've got a special project for you. Sit down."

Sherri sat in the chair Billie had just vacated.

"You might have noticed that Donald is a bit tired, down in the dumps."

Sherri nodded.

"We're entering an important phase in the primary campaign. We need him up, on top of his game, fresh. So we need to work on his psychology."

Sherri crossed her legs, rested her pad on her knee and held her pencil in position to start writing. "How do we do that?"

"No notes for this. Donald can't know we're working on him or it won't work."

"Okay."

"What I want you to do is flirt with him a little, flatter him, be subtle."

Sherri face fell. She looked at Evelyn quizzically. "You want me to—"

Evelyn held up her hands in the "stop" gesture. "Nothing physical. I want to be completely clear about that. Nothing immoral or improper. Just add a little bounce to his step."

"Like a nice guy on a date who I'm not going home with."

"Well, Sherri, I'm a little older than you, so I don't know how far that would be. Nothing physical or immoral. If your boyfriend isn't insanely jealous, this shouldn't bother him."

She nodded. "I can do that."

"You can't tell anyone. Not even Robyn or Gail or Dan or Stephen. Because if Donald finds out, even accidentally, it won't work."

She stood up. "Anything else?"

"No." Evelyn shook her head. "Thanks, Sherri, that's a load off my mind."

Sherri turned to leave.

"Oh, Sherri, best not have your boyfriend pick you up here for a while."

"No problem."

Evelyn watched Sherri walk back to her desk. She hadn't crossed any lines with what she told her, but whatever happened now was dependent upon how far Sherri would go, push comes to shove, and how she would react if Donald misinterpreted her interest and put his hands on her. Evelyn shook her head. So much for her feminist credentials. God, what a mess. Donald was a time bomb with an unreadable timer. At some point, he was going to blow himself up and everyone associated with him was going to be collateral damage. And no one knew when that was going to be, so everyone who really knew what was happening just acted as if they were going to be in the clear when the inevitable occurred.

Billie came out of Del Rey Shoes with two large bags. It was almost five o'clock. The downtown sidewalks and the city streets were busy with office workers and courthouse employees going home. Billie had not been able to make up her mind about which shoes she wanted to buy and the manager at Del Rey — they'd been on cheer squad together in high school — always let her take shoes home to try on. When she got to her car, as she reached in her handbag to press the fob to open the trunk, she heard someone behind her say, "Let me help you with that."

She smiled her plastic public smile. "I'm fine."

The trunk lid shot up. She set the bags inside and closed the trunk. When she turned, she was facing George Harrison. The lower part of his eyes still had a yellowish, greenish-purple tinge, and his nose was still lightly taped. "What a coincidence," he said. "I was just thinking about you."

"Get out of my way."

"But we have so much in common."

"I'll scream."

George took a step back. "Whoa, ma'am. You've got nothing to fear from me. This is purely an accidental encounter, unlike me running into your brother-in-law. I was just at the Price-Right Drugs across the street."

"So why did you bother to cross the street?"

"When I saw you come out of the shoe store, it suddenly occurred to me that we might have a convergence of interests."

"Hardly likely."

"For example, you'd like to get rid of my wife and I'd like to keep her, as crazy as that sounds."

Billie glanced around at the people passing on the sidewalk. "Let's get in the car."

They got into the front seats. "Okay," she said. "Say what you've got to say."

"Question number one. What would you pay for us to leave town and never be heard from again?"

"I didn't think your wife wanted to leave town."

"It's still my question. You never can tell if a person might change her mind for the right number."

"With a verified abortion?"

"You better make it two numbers, then."

"With the abortion, two hundred thousand. Without?" She shrugged. "Without the abortion, I've got no confidence I won't be bleeding money for the rest of my life. I might be persuaded to pay fifty thousand, if I could be convinced nothing would come up during the election."

"I admire a woman who knows what she wants and is willing to pay," George said. "I'll be in touch." He opened the car door.

"What do you plan to do?"

"I'm not sure yet. But I'm going to think of something fast." He got out and shut the door behind him. Billie started her car and pulled out into traffic. She needed to get home to finish off dinner and now she was running late. Had she just wasted her time? The proposition seemed too good to be true. She wouldn't hold her breath. But if Harrison did manage to pull it off, her life would be completely back to normal. What would she really be willing to pay for that? Of course, Donald would be prickly and short-tempered for a while, whining about his lost baby, but he'd get over it. He'd get busy with his life. The campaign would fill up his days. They'd move to Washington. Another woman would come along, and he'd be his old, happy-go-lucky self.

10: Choices

Over the next several days, whenever Honeycutt was at the campaign office, he noticed that Sherri was a lot friendlier than she had been previously. Whenever she brought something to him, she came up closer than she used to. In talking, she might touch his arm or pat his hand. Whenever he spoke, it seemed as though she hung on his every word, nodding and smiling. And she seemed to be showing more cleavage and wearing more perfume. It was as if she'd become his personal puppy dog, wagging her tail and chasing after him whenever he came through the door. At first he thought it was his imagination. But then he noticed that the other interns, especially the women, seemed a little taken aback by her intimacy. And the strange thing was that Evelyn wasn't doing anything about it, except acting as if she didn't notice, which meant what? That she and Billie were up to something, something that involved him sleeping with Sherri. Otherwise, Sherri would have gotten one warning, and if she hadn't change her behavior, she simply would have disappeared, to be replaced at his shoulder by the stand-offish, always correct Robyn.

Honeycutt shifted on his barstool and motioned to the bartender. He'd have one more beer and then he'd get out of here before the after-work crowd started filing in. So Billie wanted him to fuck Sherri, which meant that she was trying to move him off of Roslyn. She was never going to quit. She wanted his baby dead and Roslyn gone no matter what she said. She couldn't have a baby, so she didn't want him to have one, either. That was her brand of selfishness. All she wanted was her own way. That's all she ever wanted. And that's what this running for Congress was really about. Making her happy. Being her puppet. The closer the primary got, the less he cared about it. Oh, he still wanted to win, but his baby was more important. If she thought he would let anyone get between him and his baby, she had another thing coming.

Honeycutt drank his beer and looked off through the window at the traffic on Elm Street. His life would be so much simpler if Billie and Harrison were out of the picture. Him, his son and Roslyn. And Billie's money. He smiled bitterly. That really was another requirement, wasn't it? With Billie's money, their lives would be set—private schools, international vacations. Without Billie looking over his shoulder, he could quit the bank. He took another drink. It was the plot to a bad movie. He could pay Harrison to kill Billie. And why not? She was the one who wouldn't play fair, wanted his son dead, wasn't willing to change. Harrison would take the fall. He, on the other hand, would have his family. It was terrible even to think about. Billie was his wife. He really did love her, even with all her faults. But she was making him choose between her and his son. She was probably plotting right now to have the boy killed. So to make sure his son was going to be safe, she had to go. And if he got rid of Billie, he needed Roslyn so that his son would have a mother. That would be the easiest and the best. So Harrison had to go, too. He finished his beer. It was crazy thinking, even though it made him feel better. Just crazy thinking. As long as he didn't say any of it out loud, it wasn't real.

In the sheriff's office, Deputy Gruber sat with a file folder in his lap. "So the tire tracks I cast seem to match Bridgestone Potenza tires, which are original equipment for a lot of full-size cars." He took a photo of the casts out of the folder and passed it across the desk to the sheriff.

The sheriff put on his black-framed glasses and studied the photo, which showed two sets of slightly mashed, grayish tire treads that looked at if they'd been stripped off of their respecttive tires. "That's a lot of cars."

"Yeah, but there were a couple of cuts in the tread. Look at the lower right on the left cast and the middle of the right cast."

The sheriff nodded. "So you're saying these casts came from the same tire?"

"Yeah, the state expert says they match. Not that it would hold up in court, but it's probably the same vehicle."

The sheriff passed the photo back to the deputy. "Make some good copies. We'll distribute them to all the deputies. If they pull over a suspect, they can check the tires for a match. It's a long shot, but it's a start."

Honeycutt sat in the parking lot of the Harrisons' apartment, parked under a maple tree where he could watch their front door. It was a beautiful spring afternoon. He felt a little sleepy from the beer he'd drunk earlier. A group of four men—gray hair, windbreakers and ball caps—were on the golf course next to the parking lot getting out of their golf cart to play the green, but he couldn't recognize any of them. He turned his attention back to the Harrisons' door. He wasn't sure why he'd driven over here. He just had a feeling that this was the place he needed to be, that there was something that he needed to do here that he couldn't do anywhere else. Roslyn left the apartment dressed in black yoga pants and a light blue jacket and carrying a gym bag. She looked good. The wind was in her hair and she had a strong, healthy stride. She was his future, at least for the time being. He had to protect her if he was going to protect his baby. He slid down in his seat while he watched her get in her car and drive away. Was her husband in the apartment? He was a gigantic loose end, a giant red flashing button. He was greedy and manipulative and he had power over Roslyn. Some-thing had to be done about him. Honeycutt had to find a way to break his power. Was that why he'd come here? He got out of his car and went over to the apartment. The golfers were getting back into their cart. He rang the doorbell. George answered the door. His eyes were nearly back to normal, but his nose was still taped. "Roslyn isn't here."

"I know. I watched her leave. I came here to talk with you."

"So talk."

"You going to invite me in?"

George shrugged. "Sure. Come on in." He stepped out of the way so that Honeycutt could enter. "You want a soda, glass of water?"

"No, thanks."

"Okay, now that we're done with that, what do you want?"

Honeycutt glanced around at the furnishings. "Rent-to-own?"

George sat down on the sofa. "Is there a point in there somewhere?"

"Look, you're not Roslyn's husband, not in the normal sense of the word. You're really just business partners. You know she's going to stay with me. I've got money, power—I'm the baby daddy. So you're going to be leaving at some point, if for no other reason than you're going to get bored."

"And you've been up late at night worried about me?"

"You might as well leave with something."

"What you got in mind?"

"I'll give you twenty thousand dollars if you pack your bags and disappear."

"I was thinking of a number far north of that."

Honeycutt chuckled. "The sheriff didn't intimidate you at all, did he?"

George shook his head. "His limits are well within my tolerances."

"So what's your number?"

"One hundred thousand."

Honeycutt sat on the arm of the chair across the coffee table from George. He felt almost as if he were in a dream. Words came out of his mouth, but he didn't feel like he was thinking them first. "That's a lot of money. A person would have to earn that money."

George cocked his head. "How would I do that?"

"You want what's best for Roslyn? You want her to live happily ever after? Big house, beautiful family, happy marriage? I can provide all that."

"Doesn't sound like you need me."

"Billie's standing in the way. She's probably planning to harm Roslyn right now. If she were out of the picture, Roslyn

123

could divorce you and marry me. If you two really are married."

"Why don't you just divorce Billie? That's what most people do."

"You think that would stop her?"

"Now your reasoning sounds a lot like mine."

"A hundred thousand could take you a long way."

"You're just talking crazy."

"Maybe. Maybe I am. Maybe you don't want a hundred thousand."

"We're done here."

Honeycutt stood up and turned toward the door. His hands were shaking. He knew what he'd said — he'd wanted to say it — but he couldn't quite believe the words had come out of his mouth. He'd gone completely over the line. If Billie found out what he'd said and she believed it, she'd never trust him again. She'd do everything she could to ruin him. He'd just put his life in the hands of a man who had no reason to help him and plenty of reasons to hurt him. There was no turning back.

After Honeycutt left the apartment, George went to the window, pulled back the curtain, and watched him get in his Cadillac and drive away. Then he turned and looked at the room, trying to see it with Honeycutt's eyes. *What an arrogant, self-centered bastard. Ask your rival to murder your wife so that you can steal his wife.* Honeycutt's proposition was completely off the rails. He was right about one thing, though. Roz was slipping away from him. The baby had come completely out of left field. At first it had been a surprise, then a bargaining chip. But now it represented security, ease, even love. George couldn't compete with that. She was already beginning to think that she would stay. He knew that. But until she told him, he still had a chance. He went into the kitchen and got a Diet Coke out of the refrigerator. Did he love her enough to keep her if she kept the baby? She wouldn't be able to work much. They'd have to find a new girl to distract the suckers. But Roz could train her. And the new girl could babysit the kid when Roz worked. They'd need to do more jobs in a year. Find more amateur crooks to steal from. But maybe he'd like being a dad. He drank from the can.

The details were always a bitch. So, get the $100,000 from Honeycutt, get Roz, and skip town. And Billie's $50,000. Might as well take that too. The baby would be born before the money ran out. We'd worry about the future when it got here. He took another drink. Roz was still his girl. She'd buy into it. He just had to get her out of here before it was too late.

Jessup walked into the A-1 Diner, the truck stop out by the interstate on the south side of town. The bell rang when he came through the door. The tables were full as well as the stools at the counter. One of the servers, who was standing at the cash register, said, "It will be a few minutes, Hon. We got busy all of a sudden."

He nodded, looked around in the cacophony of small talk, cutlery on plates, chairs scraping, and waitresses taking orders, until he noticed Deputy Gruber, dressed in his sheriff's uniform, sitting alone reading a report. "I think I found a place."

He made his way to the deputy's table. "Marvin, can I join you?"

"Stan. Didn't see you come in. Sit down, sit down."

"Thanks. How you doing?"

"I'm good. Wish I was eating at home."

"I wish I had someone to cook at home."

Their waitress, a young woman with a light brown ponytail and a food-stained apron, brought him a glass of water and a menu. "Something to drink?"

"Coffee, please."

She went away.

"What you working on there?" Jessup asked.

"Just reading over the reports on the robberies out around the lake since January."

"Making any headway?"

"Not as much as I'd like. I feel like if I could just catch a break, I could solve them and maybe get a promotion."

"That's right. There's that chief deputy's spot open."

"Yeah, but the sheriff isn't in a big hurry to fill it. Wants to see results first."

The waitress brought Jessup's coffee and refilled Deputy Gruber's.

"So you're going over the reports to see if anything jumps out at you."

"That's about the size of it."

Jessup sipped his coffee. "Well, my offer still stands. You come in with me, and you'll increase your salary on the first day. Ten years from now, you'll be making half again as much as you would working for the county."

"But I won't get to be sheriff."

"No, you won't get to be sheriff."

Their waitress came back. She looked down at Jessup. "You ordering food?"

He nodded. "Give me the hamburger steak, French fries, house salad with Thousand Island."

"Coming right up."

Jessup turned back to Deputy Gruber. "Got any leads?"

"Between you and me? I've got matching tire molds from two break-ins, but that's it."

"So if you catch somebody on a new job, you might be able to fit them for the old jobs as well."

He shrugged.

"Well, maybe you'll see something new in those files."

The deputy's food came—fried chicken, French fries, and applesauce—followed shortly by Jessup's. They chatted about family, which intermural city league softball team was going to be the best, what the DNR lady had said about the probable quality of the fishing in the bend of the river on the other side of the interstate bridge, and the possibility of the Randal Junction Gun Club raising the money to build an indoor range. "That's a lot of candy bars and raffles," the deputy said.

"They need a big donor or two to kick it off."

"It's still a lot of money."

"Well, it doesn't affect you, does it? You've got the police range."

"Give me a call, and I'll slip you in with me. You know Jamie, don't you? He won't care as long as you're there with a cop." The deputy pushed his plate away.

Their waitress came over carrying the coffee pot. "More coffee?"

"No, thanks."

She turned to Jessup. He shook his head. She pulled their checks out of her apron pocket, glanced at them, and set them in front of each of them. "Thank you," she said.

The deputy glanced at his watch. "Got to go." He pushed back out of his chair. "Give me a call about the shooting range."

"Appreciate it," Jessup said.

Jessup sipped his coffee as he watched the deputy pay at the cash register — or appear to pay, looked as if the restaurant was comping his meal. Marvin was a good guy, smart, he probably would be sheriff someday. And he wouldn't be at all surprised if Marvin found a way to blow the break-ins wide open. He thought about the money Harrison had paid him. It was thoroughly laundered, but he needed to create as much distance between himself and Harrison as he could. Good thing he'd already pulled the GPS tracker off of the Avalon. He glanced at his check, left enough tip to cover Marvin and himself, paid at the cash register, and went out in to the parking lot. The evening had cooled off with the dark. A chilly breeze was stirring. He got into his Camry. He had to call Billie Honeycutt. He might be missing a chance to have sex with her one more time, but using the GPS tracker had been illegal. He had to protect her, and himself. He started his car and got out his phone. "Ms. Honeycutt? It's Stan Jessup."

"I'm busy right now. Can I call you back?"

"Just a quick word. I've got reason to believe that the sheriffs might find your friends on an unrelated bit of business. So I'm pulling the plug to avoid any unpleasantness or publicity."

"What kind of business?"

"The less you know; the better off you are."

"That kind of business? Okay. Shut it down."

"Thanks for the opportunity."

"We'll talk later."

Jessup hung up and then dialed Cindi Butler. "Cindi? Stan. Where are you?"

"I'm at home, of course. What can I do for you?"

"We're done with the Honeycutt job. You know where I hid the tracker on Honeycutt's car?"

"Yeah."

"Can you find his car and pull the tracker right now?"

"I'm cleaning up my kitchen, Stan."

"I know, I know. But wait until you see the bonus on this job. I can't go myself. Just pull the tracker and wipe the area for fingerprints."

"What's up, Stan?"

"Nothing, thus far. I just want to keep it that way."

"I'm on my way."

Jessup pulled out of the parking lot and drove back into town. Should he go to the sheriff next? He didn't want to over-play his hand. But if he turned them in, it would certainly make it hard to believe that they had paid him off. The traffic was light all the way to Elm Street. He turned toward the down-town. The tricky part was the questions that the sheriff might ask. And how he might ask them. Jessup wouldn't be able to avoid a direct answer to a direct question. At the same time, the sheriff wouldn't want to expose Billie to any trouble. So that was the flag Jessup had to drape himself in. That was his best bet. He pulled into a visitor's space at the county jail, went to reception, and asked for the sheriff.

Sheriff Teardale was standing behind his desk when the deputy who was manning reception escorted Jessup into his office. "Thanks, Tom," the sheriff said.

"Have a seat, Mr. Jessup." The sheriff indicated the office chair facing his desk.

"I think I better close the door."

The sheriff nodded. Jessup closed the door and sat down.

"I'm a busy man," the sheriff said.

"Okay. I've been doing some work for Billie Honeycutt regarding her husband, which I'd prefer not to get into."

"We'll see."

"Then I happened to run into Deputy Gruber at the A-1. We're old buddies, and he happened to mention a case he was working on—break-ins out by the lake? Matching tire tracks?"

"And?"

"After I spoke with him, it jarred my memory. It seems that George Harrison's Avalon was out in the lake area around the times of those break-ins."

"Around the time or on the days?"

"Well, I—"

The sheriff sat back in his chair and smiled. "Hypothetically, if a person was using an illegal tracking device, they would know where a car was at a particular time on a particular day."

"Correct."

"And, even though that information couldn't be used in court, it would certainly focus the attention of anyone investigating those break-ins."

"Exactly."

"So you're here because of…?"

"Overlap. Wanting to avoid contamination for my employer."

"You tell Deputy Gruber about your suspicions?"

"No, sir. Thought I should respect the chain of command."

"Anything else to add?"

"No, sheriff."

"Keep this to yourself."

"No problem."

The sheriff stood up. "Thanks for your help."

Jessup got up. He looked at the sheriff, but he didn't meet the sheriff's gaze. "I can find my way out."

"Just down the hall and to your right."

Jessup was buzzed through at the door to reception and went back out to the parking lot. So far, so good. The sheriff hadn't dug into the illegality of the GPS trackers. Jessup had inoculated himself against suspicion in the break-ins, and he might have even helped Ms. Honeycutt in the bargain. Whatever George and Roslyn Harrison were up to in the long run, they weren't going to get as far with it from the inside of a jail cell. He took out his phone. There was a voice mail from Cindi. "Stan, I've got the tracker and I wiped down the car. Do you want both trackers cleared?"

Jessup deleted the voice mail and wrote a text message. "Delete the memory and pull the batteries for good measure. Thanks."

George and Roslyn were sitting in their living room with their feet on the coffee table watching a singing competition show on TV. The contestants were all singing country songs from the 1980s, each contestant taking a turn, and no one had done very well thus far. George and Roslyn had eaten takeout Chinese for supper, and now Roslyn was sipping at a Diet Sprite and George was nursing a beer. She looked relaxed and contented, sitting there, one hand resting on her still tight abdomen. They'd had a great evening talking about nothing, just sharing each other's company, but all George could think about when he looked at her was the future. Her leaving him, staying here to keep her baby, and how he could stop her. Gambling. That's what he did for a living. But gambling wasn't about luck, or taking risks: it was about managing risk and controlling enough elements of the situation so that the elements he couldn't control were small enough that the percentages added up. Ten percent, 20 percent risk. He could work with that. But what were the percentages here? Once he had Honeycutt's money, Honeycutt was screwed. He couldn't tell anyone that he'd hired someone to kill his wife and they'd cheated him. No, the risk here was simply whether or not Roslyn would come with him, and he wouldn't know that until he showed her the money. In her current mental state, she wouldn't change her mind based on a promise. So if he really wanted to keep her, if he wasn't just playing mind games with himself, he needed to take the next step. He made a show of looking at his watch. "Oh, Roz, I almost forgot. I've got a little thing I've got to do. I'll be back in a bit."

"Wait until the show is over and I'll go with you."

He shook his head. "Sorry, baby, you can't come with me. We've got to keep you in the clear right now. If something goes wrong, it can't fall on you."

She paused the show and grabbed his arm. "I don't like the sound of that. I don't want you doing anything foolish."

"Nothing's going to happen. I'm just taking precautions."

"Then tell me where you're going."

"Can't do it." He brushed her hands off his arm. "Everything's going to be fine. Trust me." He kissed her and got up. "Watch your show. I'm just going to a meeting. I'll be back before you know it."

He slipped on a jacket and walked out to his Avalon. Once in the car, he got out his phone. "Donald? You know who this is.

We need to meet. How about the Shop-N-Save on Simmons? I'm on my way."

When George pulled into the Shop-N-Save parking lot, he could see Honeycutt's white Cadillac parked in the far corner of the parking lot among the employee cars. He stopped behind a dark blue minivan, got a palm-size audio recorder out of the glove box, turned in on, and set it under his seat. Then he drove up behind Honeycutt, tapped his horn, and unlocked his car doors. Honeycutt scurried back to the Avalon and got in. "So? What's up?"

George drove over to the nearest empty spot and pulled in. "Open your coat and lift up your shirt."

"What? Are you crazy?"

"Do it or get out."

Honeycutt unzipped his blue fleece jacket and lifted up his shirt. George reached over and felt around his sides, which made the loose skin jiggle.

"Satisfied?" Honeycutt said.

"Thanks. I just like to be careful. It's a habit you'll appreciate more over the next few days."

Honeycutt smiled. "You've been thinking about my offer. I promise you, you won't regret it."

"I'll be the judge of that. Have you got the hundred thousand?"

"I can get it by tomorrow or the next day."

"Does she have to be killed a certain way?"

"You know, really, I'd prefer not to talk about it, you know what I mean? I still love her. If it wasn't for the baby —"

George studied Honeycutt's face in the dim light coming from a nearby streetlight. He looked as if he really did mean what he said. It was a good thing that George wasn't planning on going through with it. Honeycutt already looked so guilty that he would probably confess before his wife even got to the morgue. Certainly before the funeral. Even if the coroner wrote it up as the perfect accident. What a chump. All he was good for was ripping off. "I understand."

"When will you do it?"

"When I have the money."

"Half first. Half after."

"No way. Once the deed is done, you've got no incentive to pay me."

"But once you've got the money, you've got no incentive to do the job."

"Somebody's got to trust somebody. You want me to do the job, then you've got to trust me."

"Yeah, but if I don't pay you, you could always kill me."

"How stupid do you think I am? I start dropping bodies around here, and I end up on death row. No, no, no. My plan is to leave here clean. I need cash to get set up; you're keeping Roslyn; I need to find a new partner. What are Roslyn and the baby worth to you? If they're worth a hundred thousand, pay me, and I'll get the job done. Otherwise, get out of the car and go look for someone else."

"Okay, okay," Honeycutt said, "I'll get the money. Let me think."

George took a deep breath and sat back in his seat with his hands on the steering wheel. Candy from a baby. Honeycutt didn't know how lucky he was that Roslyn wasn't going to be staying with him. She'd have him so tied up that he'd be doing what she wanted and thinking it was his own idea. The lesson George was giving him by taking his money was a public service.

"I'll meet you tomorrow at three o'clock at the Wal-Mart parking lot. I should have the money by then. If not, I'll give you a call."

"No information on the phone."

"Okay." Honeycutt zipped up his jacket, got out of the Avalon, and walked back to his own car. George watched him drive away. He reached under his seat for the audio recorder, played back the recording, and put the recorder into his pocket. Insurance. What did he need to do to leave town? Pack the clothes. Clear their bank accounts. Roslyn's Lincoln was leased, so they could leave it behind. And then there was Billie's $50,000. He'd call her in the morning. There was no reason to leave money lying on the table. He started his car and pulled out of his space. How softly did he need to go with Roslyn? That was the only thing he really needed to think about.

The next day was overcast, threatening rain. Dark clouds rolled through on gusty winds, making the temperature seem cooler than it really was. George sat with Billie in her Audi in the parking behind Jeff's Burgers. Black dirt was stuck to the greasy edges of the gray steel back door, and flattened boxes were stacked in a lopsided pile next to the dented green Dumpster. The drive-through lane was empty. The breakfast rush was over and the early lunch crowd was still an hour away. Billie scrutinized his face, looking for the lie. "You're leaving?"

"Yes."

"Both of you?"

"Absolutely."

"The fetus?"

"I don't know what's going to happen there. You said fifty thousand to get out of town."

"When are you leaving?"

"Within the next few days."

Billie got out her checkbook.

"What are you doing? I operate in a cash economy."

"I write you a check. You don't leave, I put a stop on it, and it bounces. That's how we're doing this."

George rubbed his nose where the tape had been. His nose was healing nicely, though the heat blasting through the car made it throb.

Billie tore the check out of her checkbook and handed it to him. "I hope never to see you again."

Raindrops splattered the windshield. "Pleasure doing business." George popped open the car door, pulled up the hood on his raincoat, and sprinted through the quickening shower to his own car, parked around the far side across from the drive-up window. Easy money. Now all he had to do was wait until three o'clock.

Honeycutt had spent the morning cashing in CDs from various banks around town and taking the proceeds in cash. It couldn't be helped. He couldn't take $100,000 from their main accounts at his bank, particularly in cash, without setting off alarms throughout the staff. They'd think Billie had been kidnapped, or that he was engaged in a payola scandal, or that he was being blackmailed — all of which would draw too much attention. One of the senior staff might even call Billie if he thought Honeycutt needed an intervention. No, he could have none of that. He'd had to pay penalties and lose interest, but now he had the money and Billie would never find out because she would be gone. The best way would be if she simply disappeared while he was at work. He'd have control her money, and he'd be able to postpone a marriage to Roslyn because he wouldn't be able to prove that Billie was dead.

As he hurried toward his car, the rain started up again. He pressed "unlock" on the car key fob, reached for the car door handle, and saw his shadowy reflection in the driver's door window. Was he really going to hire Harrison to kill Billie? He could still back out, go to Billie, have a heart to heart, maybe she would soften her stance. He put the briefcase full of money into the backseat and got into the driver's seat. But Billie would say anything. She'd already proven that. There was only one way to guarantee the safety of his baby. He was going to have to give Billie up. She was going to have to go. Otherwise he would always have to be on guard, watching her, watching out for his son, protecting him from his wicked stepmother.

When Honeycutt pulled into the Wal-Mart parking lot at 3:00 p.m., George was already waiting in his Avalon in the far corner of the lot, away from the security cameras. Honeycutt pulled up beside him. He waited for a moment for the rain to slow down; then he reached back into the backseat for the briefcase, hurried over to George's car, and got into the passenger's seat.

"We still on?" George asked.

Honeycutt tapped on the briefcase. "That sound empty?"

"Give it here."

Honeycutt passed George the briefcase. He opened it and looked at the bundles of bills. "Very nice."

"When?"

"Very soon. You don't want to know. Forget about this meeting. Keep a full schedule. It happens when it happens. It's got nothing to do with you."

Honeycutt nodded his head. He opened his mouth as if he were going to say something, but then he realized he had nothing to say. He rushed through the rain back to his own car, while George Harrison drove away. Honeycutt sat in his car watching the rain bounce off his windshield and his windows start to fog. What had he done? Why had Billie made him do this? Why couldn't she have just loved his baby? It would have been so much easier. But that was the flaw in her character. She only had room in her heart for people who helped her get what she wanted. All the time they'd spent together and all the time they were going to spend together. The past and the future. Here, Washington, who knew where else? Gone because of the choice she made. And yet, his chest hurt as if he'd been down in the water too long and couldn't take a breath. He started his car. After all she'd done to try to kill his son, why did he still love her so much?

George drove into the concrete parking deck at the Junction Center Mall, the shopping mall at the east end of Simmons Boulevard, and drove up to the second level, where Roslyn was waiting in a parking space across from the mall entrance. George found a nearby spot and walked over to her Lincoln with the briefcase in his hand. "Hey, honey." He slammed the car door as he sat down. The sound echoed through the concrete structure.

Roslyn leaned over and kissed him. "What's up? What did you want to meet about?"

George opened the briefcase in his lap.

"What's this?"

"This is our traveling money. A hundred fifty thousand. I thought you'd like to buy some new clothes before we left town."

She glanced from George to the cash and back to George, her face tightening. "How did you get it?"

"Marital discord. Billie gave us fifty thousand to leave town. George gave me a hundred thousand to kill Billie."

"So George is going to choose me over her." She smiled, but her eyes couldn't hide their empty, calculating look.

"George has convinced himself he's choosing the baby. He's been weepy all along the way, like he really loves his wife but has to betray her. Who knows how long he's going to last before his guilt gets the best of him?"

"And what's your plan?"

George looked at her carefully. Now he knew that he was going to have to sell her hard. "I'm with you however you want to roll. You want to keep your baby? Fine. You want to quit working jobs and help me train someone new? Great. I've never thought of myself as a father, but if that's what you want, I'll give it all I've got. I'm here for you, honey. It's me and you forever."

Roslyn's eyes filled with tears. "God, I'm crying and I don't know why. It must be the hormones."

George took her hand. "It's just us. Me and you against all comers."

"And the baby."

"Me and you and the baby against all comers."

She dabbed at her cheeks with a tissue. An odd gleam lit up her eyes. "And we're going to be on the road, living in hotel rooms and rented apartments, me and you and my baby and the new girl."

"Just me and you."

"A girl younger and prettier than me who we're going to turn out to hustle marks, who I'm going to teach all my tricks to, all the tricks you love, all the tricks she'll have to practice on you." Tears ran down her face.

"It won't be like that."

She scrunched up the tissue in her fist. "And then you won't need me anymore."

He shook his head. "Roslyn. No. I love you. It'll always be me and you. Me and you and the baby. Nobody could ever come between us."

"I'm not leaving."

"How's that going to work? I'm not killing Billie Honeycutt."

"I don't care." She pushed out of the car, stumbled to her feet, and scurried toward the mall entrance.

George shut the briefcase, set it on the floor mat, and started after her. What could he tell her to get her out of here, to get her down the road to the next place, to get her to somewhere where she could start making sense? "Roslyn," he called after her, "listen to me."

She went into the mall, walking fast, *clickity-click* on her high heels, her tan raincoat flapping behind her, and turned into the J.J. Barnes Department Store. George was trying to catch up, trying to move as fast as he could without running, without attracting attention. "Roslyn," he called after her, "tell me how you want it to be. Tell me what we need to do."

She didn't even look over her shoulder. She got on the escalator. He jogged a few steps and then started walking up the escalator after her. He caught up to her just as she reached the top. He grabbed her by both arms. He whispered. "Tell me, Roz, tell me how it's supposed to be and I'll make it that way."

"Let go of me." She knocked his arms loose. "Can't you see, Georgie, you can't make things that way I want them to be. No matter what you say, it's not in you."

"Roz, please, listen." She started to step away, but her raised foot glanced into his leg, her weight shifted, and the narrow heel of the high heel shoe she was standing on began to pivot. It was as if it were all happening in slow motion. She started to fall backward. George spun around and grabbed for her shoulder, her arm, her hand, but she was gone. Her head hit the handrail, and she bounced down the up escalator, banging against the stainless steel sides until she came to rest at the bottom, George chasing her all the way but never quite reaching her. She was unconscious. Her face was blood and bruises. There was blood soaking into her dress. He cradled her in his arms while a few shoppers and a cosmetics counter employee rushed over. "Call an ambulance!" he yelled. "Call an ambulance!" He looked down in her face. "Oh, baby, oh baby, oh baby. I'm here. I'm here." There was blood on his hands. Tears ran down his cheeks. "I'll fix this. I'll fix this. I never should have let this happen to you."

11: Repercussions

It was morning before Honeycutt found out that Roslyn had been in an accident. He and Billie were eating breakfast at the granite countertop that separated their kitchen from their family room. Honeycutt was already dressed for the office, while Billie was still in her sleep shirt and fluffy blue robe. The local morning news show was playing on the TV in the family room. The strawberry-blonde newsreader reported the accident at the J.J. Barnes Department Store on the previous evening. "What's that?" Honeycutt turned up the volume with the remote. Roslyn had fallen down the escalator in what police investigators were describing as a freak accident. She was in stable condition at Tri-County Medical Center. "My God." The color drained from his face. He turned off the TV.

"J.J. Barnes. That's a tall escalator," Billie said. She squeezed his hand. "But she's in stable condition, and they didn't say anything about the baby, so she must be okay."

Honeycutt nodded his head. "You're probably right. She'll probably be fine in a few days." He pushed his over-easy eggs and buttered toast away. "I can't finish this."

"You should go straight to the hospital. Park in the small lot off Mitchell Street and use the back elevator. That way you won't be seen."

"That's a good idea."

"Do you want me to go with you?"

"No, I should do this on my own."

"Then get going. You need facts. Worrying about hypotheticals won't help."

"You're right. Worrying won't help." When he got to the kitchen door to the garage, he turned. "Thanks for being so supportive. I know how hard all this is for you. I love you."

She smiled. "I love you, too." She sipped her coffee and looked out the family room windows at the bird feeders. She heard the garage door go up and then down. Who owed her a favor in administration at the medical center? Someone who could look at computerized patient records. Someone capable and reliable. Tammy Juarez. She picked up her phone.

George walked into Roslyn's room at the medical center carrying a bouquet of flowers from Gerard's, the high-end flower shop downtown. He'd spent the night sitting in the chair in her room, hoping to talk with her, but she'd been asleep ever since the nurses brought her out of surgery. Even though he'd gone home to shower and change clothes, he still looked as if he'd been on a two-week bender: gray face, red-rimmed eyes, a slight tremor in his hands. She was lying on her back covered by a thin, baby blue hospital blanket, her reddish-brown hair sticking out in odd directions, her left arm lying out to expose the IV lines connected to a bag of fluids. As he approached the bed, she turned her face toward him, and whispered, "What are you doing here?"

He smiled. "I'm so glad you're awake, Roz. I was here all night. I just went home to change. I brought you some flowers."

"Throw them away. I don't want anything from you. Get out of here and leave me alone."

He set the flowers on the counter. "I'm here to help. Whatever you need."

She coughed, and then scrunched up her face as if her guts hurt. "I can't talk any louder than this. Get out."

"Baby—"

She pressed the button for assistance. "You pushed me. Get out. Get out. Get out."

A nurse, a middle-aged Latina with gray-streaked hair pulled back in a tight bun, entered the room. Roslyn looked toward her. "Make him leave."

"You have to leave, sir."

"I'm her husband."

The nurse shook her head and motioned toward the door. She followed him into the hall. "We can't have her upset. After surgery sometimes a person may be confused. Get some rest, have something to eat, come back later. We have your contact information?"

"Yeah. I filled out the papers last night."

"Then go home. She's safe now. Every hour she is just going to get better."

A short time later, Honeycutt stepped out of the elevator at the back of the medical center and made his way through the labyrinth of halls until he found Roslyn's room. He tapped lightly on the door and went in. The TV was tuned to a morning news show, one of the ones he wasn't familiar with, though the sound wasn't loud enough to be distinct. Roslyn lay in bed, her upper body slightly elevated. She smiled when she saw him. Her hair had been brushed and her bedding straightened up a bit, but her face was puffy and a dark bruise covered her left cheek. He reached for her right hand and gave it a gentle squeeze. "I heard what happened thirty minutes ago. How are you?"

"I'm okay," she whispered.

He sat down beside her. "How are you injured?"

"Knocked about. Some cracked ribs. Loose teeth. Concussion. Feel like I was in a car wreck."

"How long are they going to keep you?"

She shook her head. "I don't know."

"So the baby's okay?"

She gripped his hand as hard as she could. "I lost the baby."

"Lost the baby?"

"I was bleeding. Had surgery. Dr. Binder says I can still have kids, though."

He felt dizzy. His stomach churned and he tried to swallow. "Roslyn, I'm so sorry. I'm glad you're going to be okay."

"We can still get married. Have another baby."

"Was it a boy?"

"Don't know."

He patted her hand with his free hand. His beautiful son was dead. No baby to hold, no Little League champ, no college graduate. It had all been just a crazy dream. Tears started out of his eyes. He wiped them with his handkerchief. He looked at Roslyn: no makeup, no clothes, no personality. She was a middle-aged wreck. Billie was waiting at home. "Roslyn, Roslyn. You're too old to try again. It's too risky. The odds for birth defects are too steep. You know that as well as I do. I'm glad you're well." He nodded his head. "I really am. I hope you make a full recovery. But without the baby, we've got nothing in common."

"We could still be together."

"Why? To what point? I wish you the best." He pulled his hand free.

"Don't you love me?"

"Roslyn, our baby is gone. Maybe God is trying to tell us something. I've got to go." He stood up. "Good-bye."

"You can't just throw me away."

"I'm not throwing you away. Rest. We'll talk later."

He walked back down the hall, shielding his face with his hand as he passed the nurses' station. His life felt empty and pointless. Yesterday he was a father, and then suddenly today he wasn't. The world had turned upside down. All he knew for certain was that his plans were crap: his plans to save his son, his plans to get rid of Billie, his plans to marry Roslyn, his plans to live happily ever after. Maybe this really was a message from God. Maybe God wanted him to stay with Billie and go to Congress. The elevator opened. He got in and pressed "L." There was something important he needed to do, but he just couldn't remember what it was.

Roslyn lay in her bed, looking at the ceiling, silently sobbing. How had it gone so wrong? When had she lost her charm? Donald should have been down on his knees with an engagement ring. Instead, she was just the other woman, just another woman. Entirely replaceable. He'd still have to pay to avoid a scandal, but what did that matter? When had she drunk her own Kool-Aid? She'd gotten lazy, relying on the baby to do her job of being captivating and intoxicating. Even worse, she'd convinced herself that the baby would set her free, make her whole, remake her world. She wiped her face with the edge of her blanket. She exhaled deeply and lay back. How had she ended up here? It was all a blur. She remembered being in the mall parking deck. She closed her eyes. An argument with George. She jumped out of the car. She ran inside, up the escalator. J. J. Barnes. Was that real or a dream? He was chasing after her, but he wasn't angry. What was she wearing? The interior of the department store swirled around. He was there with his hands on her shoulders. She didn't want to listen to him. She knocked his hands free. She was spinning. He was reaching for her, calling her name and reaching for her. She was falling, falling. Then she was gone.

Honeycutt didn't go home after he left Roslyn at the medical center. He drove around for a while, following the grid up and down, flowing with the traffic, stopping at the lights, always turning right, not left. Finally, he pulled into a coffee shop he'd never been in before, one far off the beaten track where he hoped no one would recognize him or want to talk to him. Even though he wasn't hungry, he ordered a big breakfast—scrambled eggs, pancakes, greasy hash browns—and picked up the floater morning newspaper. His phone was vibrating. Billie was calling him. She probably already knew about the miscarriage. He didn't answer. He knew that his real life was closing in fast and that he was going to have to accept it and get on with it, but he just wasn't quite ready to hear her not gloat. His son was dead. His dreams were dead. All that was left were her dreams. His food came. He ate slowly, packing it all down, and drank two cups of coffee. Even though his life would never have meaning again like it had for the short time when he had been a father, and even though Billie was too selfish to understand such a thing unless it were her baby, she was still all that he had left in the world. He called George Harrison.

"Hey, do you know who this is?"
"Yeah."
"The deal is off."
"I thought as much."
"Can you meet me where we met before?"
"When?"
"Now."

Honeycutt had been sitting in the Wal-Mart parking lot for fifteen minutes before George arrived. The late morning traffic in and out of the store was slow, mainly moms in sweatpants with toddlers on their hips and retired guys clutching shopping lists. The morning clouds had cleared. The sun was drying the pavement. Honeycutt lowered his window. The air felt fresh. He watched a young mom put a baby riding in a baby carrier into a shopping cart. She bent down into the cart—what was she doing? Adjusting a blanket, saying a word? Then she pushed the cart toward the entrance. He felt a wave of emotion and, closing his eyes, he rested his head on his steering wheel. A car horn sounded. He looked up. George pulled in next to him and motioned for him to get into the Avalon. Honeycutt climbed into the passenger's side. George half smiled. "Sorry I'm late. There was an accident at the corner with Elm."

"You look like shit."

"Yeah, well, up all night."

"My condolences. It's been a hard twenty-four hours for both of us. As I said on the phone, the deal is off. I want my money back."

"Sorry, no refunds. I'll still kill her if you like."

"Is this really the way you want to play this?"

"I'm not playing. I'm a working guy trying to make a living. You think you just suddenly decided to hire me? I've been setting this up for months. I've got expenses, overhead, a partner fucked up in the hospital."

"What if I put the sheriff on you?"

"You are so screwed, you know that? This ain't checkers; it's chess. Any move you make now just digs you in deeper." George tapped his index finger against the side of his head. "Think it through."

"I could hire someone to kill you."

George waved him off. "Really? Who do you know? You might as well give that money to me right now. Nobody will kill anybody for you. Nobody. This is how our relationship is going to work. I'm keeping your money, and you'll keep paying the ten thousand every month if you want to keep your wife happy. 'Candidate dumps girlfriend after miscarriage.' Sounds like front page above the fold in your local rag."

Honeycutt couldn't think of anything to say.

"Cheer up. Your situation is no worse than it was to begin with. Oh, except now you pay without getting laid. Get out of my car."

"I'm not done with you."

"You are used to having your way, aren't you? How about if I earn the hundred thousand by killing you? You dumb putz, how would that work for you?"

Honeycutt looked at George's face. His eyes stared back like dead man's eyes, his face as flat as a mask. Honeycutt got out of the car. George drove away.

Honeycutt started back to his Cadillac, stopped, walked around to the front bumper, and vomited in the grass. What did he really know for a fact? Roslyn was pregnant, but was it his baby? The paternity test was coming up. She was confident. So it had to be his. But was the baby an accident or was he just part of their plan? He grabbed the fender to steady himself and spat. His stomach churned, but nothing else came up. And the miscarriage? Was that an accident or part of the plan? If it was part of the plan, then the baby wasn't his. What kind of a person would use a baby like that? It was worse than slavery. His stomach heaved. Nothing. He stood up and wiped his mouth with his handkerchief. No, Roslyn was good, she'd played him, no doubt, but she wasn't that good. She wanted that baby. He sat down in his car and found an old half-filled water bottle. He rinsed his mouth and spat out the open door. From sweet dream to nightmare, his life was back to normal. He shut the car door and drove home.

When he came into the house from the garage, Billie was waiting for him. She put her arms around him. "Poor baby," she said. "What a shock. You've been sick. I'm surprised you could drive. I called in case you needed a ride, but you didn't pick up. Go brush your teeth and I'll fix you a drink."

Billie was in the family room when he came back down, a martini in each hand. She handed one to him. "You've had a hell of a shock."

He couldn't get his mouth to work. He gulped down half the drink, took a breath, and finished it. He looked at her blankly. "Thanks."

"Where do we stand? I've already called Tri-County and taken responsibility for the medical bills."

He reached out and she handed him her drink. He took a sip. "Harrison has already told me that we've got to keep paying the ten thousand. Otherwise, so far as me and you, so far as the election, we're back on course if you'll still have me. So far as me—" his voice broke. He sat down, set the martini on the coffee table, and looked down at the carpet. "I know we can't have a funeral, but I want to do something—do something for my son."

Billie sat down next to him and rubbed his back. "Take your time. Maybe you want to set up a charity or scholarship. It would have to appear to be for some other purpose, of course, but you'd always know. We could organize fundraisers to create an endowment. Maybe something else will seem more appropriate."

He turned and looked at her. "That sounds good. You're right. I need to take my time. Think about the best way." He took a sip of the martini and passed it to her. "I fell off course. I screwed things up. But this shock brought me around. I'm back now. It's just us. Just as it should have been all along."

Billie sipped the martini. "I've been waiting for you to say that. It seems like a long time. I'm glad you're back." She combed his hair back with her hand and kissed him. "It's not too late. We can still win. We're pulling the trigger on the endorsements tomorrow."

"There's no 'can,' we're going to win." Honeycutt took the martini from her and took another sip. It seemed as if he'd convinced her. All he had to do was keep acting. Eventually, he'd convince himself.

"No more women?"

"No more women, except you."

In the early evening, George rapped gently on the door to Roslyn's hospital room before he entered. She was sitting up, looking at a *Country Home* magazine. The bruising on her face and arms had gone down considerably, and the IV had been pulled. Her hair was tied back at the nape of her neck, and someone had helped her with some lipstick. The flowers that he had brought that morning were in a vase by her bed.

"Hey, Roz."

"Hey."

"I see the flowers found water in time."

"The nurse took care of them while I was sleeping."

He walked up to the side of her bed. "You look a lot better. I was worried this morning."

She looked at him curiously, her eyes seeking, her head tilted oddly. "You didn't push me, did you?"

"Roz, when you slipped and fell and I couldn't grab you in time, I've never felt so helpless."

She sighed. "Donald stopped by. Found out about the miscarriage and gave me the kiss off. It hurt a lot more than I thought it would."

George took her hand in both of his. "It's tough, I know. It's easy to get caught up in the game, all your hopes and dreams swirling around in the toilet. I got the hundred fifty thousand, though. And we're still collecting ten grand a month."

"Oh, yeah. The money. You showed me in the car. There's so much I still can't remember. Georgie, I'm so sorry I was mean to you this morning."

"Forget about it. The only thing that matters is that you get well."

"Dr. Binder says I ought to be able to go home tomorrow."

"Really?"

"It's mainly bruises. The D and C went fine. It's just one more night of observation to be sure. She's been so kind to me."

George ran his hand along her cheek. "I'm so sorry for you, Roz. I know you really wanted the baby. I know you wanted a new life; that you think you're getting too old for our hustle. I just didn't realize how afraid you were that I'd throw you over for a new partner."

"I wasn't thinking straight."

"You're my one and only, baby. If you want the straight life, I'll help you get on your way."

"It was all a stupid dream."

"Honey, you can still have it. We'll go somewhere new. We'll use the money to set our play. Only instead of setting up a sucker, we'll be setting up a rich husband for you."

"You're so good to me, Georgie. I could never leave you. Besides, I don't know how to do anything else."

"You think about it. Whatever you want."

"I don't know what I want, except that I want to get away from here. I know it sounds crazy, but my heart is broken. Not by Donald, but by losing the baby."

George looked hard in her eyes. "So you don't care if I mess up his play?"

"Mess up his play? How?"

"He's got it coming, the way he treated you. Overprivileged, self-absorbed bastard. He's definitely got it coming."

"But you got his money."

"Not enough."

"Are you going to use the pictures?"

He shook his head. "Never. That would involve you. We can't have you in the papers or on TV."

"Then what?"

"Don't worry about it. I've got a few tricks up my sleeve. You just rest up so I can bring you home."

"Don't do anything stupid. I'm depending on you."

"The sheriff's the only muscle in this town, Roz, and I'm going to stay on his good side. You can be sure of that."

12: Tipping the Cart

The next day, while George was putting groceries into the refrigerator, Roslyn lay on the sofa in the living room watching the early news on the TV. She was dressed in gray sweatpants and a baby-blue scooped neck top. Her pink fleece robe was thrown over her legs. "That's taking a long time. How much did you buy?"

"Just a few days." He opened the freezer. "I got some of that ice cream you like. You want some?"

Roslyn turned from the TV. "I couldn't eat another thing."

"You need to build up your strength."

"You're going to fatten me up and then complain that I'm fat."

George put the ice cream and the frozen vegetables in the freezer and opened the refrigerator. "Glass of milk?"

"I'm not listening." She turned back to the TV, where she saw Honeycutt standing with a group of men. "George, quick."

He shut the refrigerator door and trotted into the room with a bag of lettuce in his hand. The newsreader's voice said, "Local banker Donald Honeycutt, candidate for the US House of Representatives, received the endorsement of a number of local politicians at the monthly Movers Club meeting at noon today." The TV showed Honeycutt shaking hands with the mayor and the sheriff and the chair of the county commission, a big confident smile on his face.

"He looks good," Roslyn said.

The newsreader switched to a different topic. George went back into the kitchen to put away the rest of the groceries." He won't look good for long. I'm going to wipe that smile off his face."

"Really, George," Roslyn said. "It's not worth it. I don't want you back in the hospital. They set the sheriff on you again, who knows what's going to happen."

"Baby, relax. I'm not going to do anything illegal in this jurisdiction. Period."

"Then why won't you tell me what you're going to do?"

"It's a surprise. I don't know how it's going to work out. Let me wave my magic wand, and then I tell you all about it." He put away the last can.

"Nothing illegal?"

He sat down beside her. "Nothing illegal. I know you're counting on me. I'm not going to let you down." He got up and put on his jacket. "I've got a meeting to go to. I'll be back in a little while. Then I'll start on dinner. You just rest."

George drove across town to the Wal-Mart, where he had set up a meeting with Billie Honeycutt. The parking lot was busy; shoppers were pushing full carts out into the lot; new arrivals were cruising the aisles hoping to find a parking spot close to the doors. But there were still plenty of spots in the far corner of the lot, which was where George found Billie. He got out of his car and climbed into her Audi. She gave him a look that managed to express both her boredom and disgust. "I'm here. What could be so important to me to bring me across town? You've failed at breaking up my marriage. You're getting paid. What is it?"

George took a small audio recorder out of his pocket. "Relax. I'm just trying to do you a favor." He turned up the volume and pressed play. His voice came out of the speaker.

"Have you got the hundred thousand?"

"I can get it by tomorrow or the next day."

"Does she have to be killed a certain way?"

"You know, really, I'd prefer not to talk about it, you know what I mean? I still love her. If it wasn't for the baby — "

He pressed stop. "Do I need to tell you who the other voice is?"

Her eyes were like a rabbit's caught in a spotlight. She looked from George to the recorder and back again. "You expect me to believe this?"

"You might think I'm a son of a bitch, but that's the man you married. Hired me to kill you over a dream that would never come true. How many years you been together?"

"If you're looking for more money, you're out of luck. I already paid you fifty thousand to get out of town."

"Actually, according to your offer, you owe me one hundred fifty thousand more, but I'm not looking for another penny. In fact, keep the recorder as a parting gift." He set the recorder on the seat.

"Get out of my sight. You and Roslyn almost wrecked all my dreams."

"Really? All your dreams?" He opened the car door. "You're living a sad, sad life. Hope the make-up sex is worth it." George shut her door carefully, got in his Avalon and drove away. He'd done everything he could to tip up Honeycutt's cart. Now it was up to Billie.

Billie sat in her car, looking out at the Wal-Mart traffic — cars pulling into empty spots, people going into the building, people coming out pushing carts of bagged up groceries, loading cars, driving away — but she wasn't seeing any of it. She rewound the recording and played it, rewound it and played it, rewound it and played it, hoping to cast doubt on her initial impression, but the words and her understanding were always the same. Donald had hired George Harrison to murder her. Even though he loved her, or claimed to, because the fetus, which hadn't even been proven to be his yet, was more important than she was. He wanted to be a father more than he wanted to be her husband, more than he wanted to be a congressman, more than he wanted a reputation as a clean-living family man. Marrying a whore to keep a baby was more important than his relationship with her. She listened again. Maybe the recording had been altered? It happened all the time in TV and the movies. She could have Jessup take it to a private lab to be tested. Keep this problem under wraps until the results came back. Take the time to watch Donald, study him, figure out if he were really capable of such a deed.

She turned off the recorder and put it in her jacket pocket. No. She knew she was grasping at straws. Harrison would only spend money to make money. He'd made the recording to use against Donald. If she'd died, Donald would've been under his thumb forever. But the fetus miscarried. Something changed in his calculations, so she lived and she got the recording. But what to do about Donald? Use the recording to keep him in line? No. Eventually she'd let down her guard and he'd go back to his old games. She'd always had a soft spot for him. She'd always be one leaky condom away from divorce or murder. She just hadn't known it. No, she had to man-up while the pain was fresh, do the smart thing no matter how much it hurt in the short run. She drove out of the Wal-Mart parking lot and headed downtown. The traffic on Elm Street was stop and go. She picked up her phone and called Bo. "Hey, I need to talk with you right away."

"You sound scared. What's the problem?"

"I'd rather talk in person. Are you at the jail?"

"I can be there in fifteen minutes."

"I'll meet you there."

Once she'd driven through the Maple Street intersection, the traffic was mainly outbound, and she sailed along. She would be at the county jail in just a few minutes, but she wasn't sure what she should do. Should she fill in Bo with what she'd learned or what she thought she'd learned? Should she just give him the recording and let him come to his own conclusions? And what did she want done? Because once she told him, there'd be no holding him back. If she didn't tell him what to do, he'd do whatever he thought was right. Was she ready for that? Divorce, scandal, good-bye Washington. The courthouse was on her left, but she didn't turn onto the courthouse square to go to the county jail. She just kept going. She picked up her phone and tapped her last call. "Bo, it's me. I changed my mind."

"You sure you don't need help?"

"I'm fine. I'll talk with you later."

"Stop by the jail anyway, just so I can see you're okay."

"I'm okay, Bo. Really."

"If you say so."

"If I need help, you'll be the first person I call."

She drove home. Mamie was shuffling about in the kitchen, stirring pots and checking the oven. Honeycutt was sitting in the family room, reading the newspaper and drinking a scotch and water. "Hey, Donny."

He set the newspaper down. "Hi, Billie, did you have a good afternoon?"

"I did. The endorsements have created a lot of excitement. Doris and her mom want to hold a house party for you. How's your drink?"

"I'm fine."

Billie poured herself a whiskey. The recording was playing in her mind. She turned to Mamie. "What's for dinner?"

"Irish stew, green beans, and fresh biscuits. Be ready in fifteen minutes."

"Thanks, Mamie. You didn't have to wait. Donald could have kept an eye out until I got home."

"Trust a man in the kitchen?"

Honeycutt smiled. "I'll never be up to her standards." He went back to reading the newspaper.

Mamie took off her apron. "I'll call my ride."

"I think your nephew is parked on the street in front of the house."

Mamie got her coat and handbag from the front hall closet. Billie walked her to the front door. "See you in the morning."

"I've got that doctor's appointment. So Chrissie will be here early."

Billie patted her shoulder. "You take care, Mrs. Peters."

Mamie smiled. "Yes, ma'am."

Billie locked the door behind her. Now she was alone with Donald. Should she be scared? She walked back into the kitchen, set down her drink, and stirred the stew. No, he couldn't kill her himself. And the baby was gone, so he didn't have a reason to want her dead. She looked at him over the kitchen island. "So how are you feeling, Donny, really?"

He laid the newspaper on the coffee table. "I'm doing a little better. If I keep busy, think about the future, you know, remind myself of the bad parts, how my behavior pulled us apart . . ." He shrugged. "Sometimes, knowing how much I hurt you is the worst part of it."

"Well, we've got each other. And we've got plenty to do. Let's not ever let something come between us like that again."

"I love you."

"I love you." She pulled the biscuits from the oven. "Supper's ready."

They ate at the kitchen island, talking amiably, sharing a bottle of merlot. Honeycutt had a good appetite, ate seconds and had ice cream for dessert. Billie wasn't hungry. She ate just enough to avoid comment. The longer she sat with him, the more she realized how much she'd misjudged his ability to lie and dissemble. She'd always known that he'd used his good looks and charm to take advantage of people. He'd chosen a fetus over her. Okay, she thought, take a breath; maybe she could live with that. Maybe she wanted him that much or maybe she wanted to someday be a senator's wife that much. Then he'd contracted her murder to seal his choice. Okay, take another breath; maybe she could chalk that up to temporary insanity. Maybe she could convince herself that it would never happen again; that he had learned his lesson. But now here he was selling her on his innocence, acting as if the worst thing he'd done was have an affair that had gotten out of hand. If she hadn't heard the recording, if the recorder wasn't in her coat pocket, she wouldn't believe that he'd actually planned to have her murdered. And knowing what she knew, maybe she could continue to sit and talk with him, maybe she could continue to plan and execute the campaign with him, maybe she could continue to carry on their shared life and pretend that he hadn't hired a man to murder her. But right then, looking into his smiling face as he reached across and patted the back of her hand, she knew that she would never be able to go up into the bedroom and spread her legs for the lying, deceiving monster sitting across from her.

Honeycutt got up to take his plate to the sink. "That was a great dinner, Bils. Be sure to thank Mamie for me."

Billie smiled. She had to get out of here before she gave herself away. "You have anything planned this evening?"

"I thought I'd check in with Evelyn and the volunteers. Do my part to keep the excitement going."

"Good idea." Billie got up, collected the rest of the dishes, and took them to the sink.

"Want to come along?"

"No, you go ahead. It's good for them to see you without me, and I've got a few chores I want to take care of before bed." She started rinsing the dishes and stacking them to put in the dishwasher.

"Okay." He came up beside her and kissed her cheek. She flinched. "Jumpy," he said.

"Thought I was going to break a glass." She turned her face and kissed him on the lips.

"See you later."

While she loaded the dishwasher, she heard the garage door go up and down. She started the dishwasher and then went up to their bedroom and packed her overnight bag, a red duffel she kept in the floor of her closet. She couldn't make love with Donald, she wouldn't sleep beside him, and she shouldn't sleep in the same house. If she stayed, she'd start to waiver. By the end of the week, she'd be convincing herself that the recording didn't mean what it seemed to mean, that she'd misunderstood, that Harrison had conned her. She went into her bathroom and got her toiletries bag. No more one step forward and two steps back. She was going to have to face the truth. She was done with Donald. There was no saving their relationship. She called Bo. "I changed my mind again."

"You're family, Billie. You can change your mind as much as you like. I'm in my office."

"I'll be there in fifteen minutes. If I don't show up, come looking for me."

"Where are you?"

"I'm at home."

"By yourself?"

"Yeah, Donald went to the campaign office."

"I'll come there."

"No, please don't. I'm on my way."

She put her toiletries bag into the red duffel, zipped it up, and went back downstairs. When she got to the kitchen, she found Honeycutt standing there. "Hi, honey," he said. "What's the bag for?"

"I thought you were going to the campaign office."

"I called on the way. No one was working this evening, so it was a waste of time."

She walked by him and set the bag down by the back door. "I've got an overnight trip tomorrow, remember? I told you about it last week. Kansas City to meet with some money people for the general election."

"Must have slipped my mind." He moved closer to her, reached into a drawer on the island, and got out a paring knife. "I know this sounds crazy, but I'm still hungry. Do we have any apples?"

"Have you looked in the fruit crisper?" She shook her head as if commenting on his inability to help himself, squeezed by him and opened the refrigerator. "Macintosh or Yellow Delicious?"

He crowded in behind her. "Yellow Delicious."

She handed him the apple and turned to shut the refrigerator door, but he didn't move. The knife in his hand was only a few inches from her side. "Did you happen to see George Harrison today?"

"George Harrison?" She shook her head. "Why? I thought you said we still had to pay him the ten thousand every month."

"Just curious." He stepped over to the sink and started peeling the apple.

Billie shut the refrigerator door. Her phone rang.

The sheriff said, "I'm on my way."

"I'm just leaving, Bo. I'll be there in a few minutes."

Honeycutt looked up at her expectantly without taking the knife away from the half-peeled apple, the skin hanging down in one long strip.

"Bo wanted to talk with me. I think he's got a girlfriend problem."

"Then you better get going."

She opened the kitchen door to the garage.

He went back to peeling the apple. "You know that George Harrison is going to try to stir things up."

"I know."

He nodded toward the red duffel lying on the floor by her feet. "Don't forget to put your bag in the car."

"What?"

"Your bag. You don't want to forget it when you're rushing around in the morning." The apple peel fell into the garbage disposal.

She picked up the duffel bag. "Thanks."

He set the knife down on the counter by the sink. "See you in a bit."

She put the duffel into the backseat of her Audi, sat down in the driver's seat and locked the doors before she raised the garage door. She could feel her heart pounding in her chest. Had he really been toying with her or was she just being paranoid? She wasn't going to find out. She wasn't coming back to this house as long as he was still living here. She backed out of the garage and down the driveway. This is what it had come to. Making her escape from her own house, the house she and Tommy had bought together. She picked up her phone. "Bo? I'm in my car and on my way."

At the sheriff's office, Billie sat across from the sheriff with a box of tissues in her lap. The audio recorder that George Harrison had given her sat on the desk between them. The sheriff was wearing his black-framed glasses and looking at the recorder, his mouth slightly open, but he hadn't spoken since the recording finished playing. Billie wiped her eyes with a wad of tissue. "So I went home, instead of coming here—I just couldn't, I hadn't finished processing, I didn't fully understand what the recording meant. But the longer I was in the house with him, the more fearful I became. I had to get out of there."

"I'm sorry, Billie. Even for me, and I've never liked him, this is hard for me to get my mind around." He looked up at her face. "You did the right thing getting out of there."

"Can you get him out of my house?"

"Oh, yeah. I'll arrest him, but this recording is not enough to convict, I don't think. Conspiracy is hard to prove, especially when your witness is a criminal."

"It'll be enough to keep him from getting any of my money in the divorce."

The sheriff took off his glasses and set them on his desk. "How hard do you want me going after him? I could arrest Harrison and his wife, the whole nine yards."

"This is so embarrassing. If all this comes out, the womanizing, the pregnancy and everything, I'll look like a complete idiot."

"Once the lawyers get started, there'll be no dirty rock left unturned. The way they'll frame your position on the pregnancy, for example. It won't be pretty."

"I would just really like to get this all behind me. Get rid of Donald, cut my losses, and move on." She sobbed. "The campaign. All my plans. Destroyed. I never would have thought a year ago that this is where I would end up. My dreams crushed. My marriage a failure. You were right all along. Why couldn't I see who he really was?"

The sheriff nodded sympathetically. "You were lonely. Grieving after Tommy passed. You needed someone. In a situation like that, a person often sees what they want to see. You aren't the first person this has ever happened to. But we're going to get this fixed up, okay? Think about this. You don't have to decide everything right this minute. Let's say the Harrisons are gone. Can't be found. You have the recording. Donald has nothing. Your options are open and there's not much he can do to hurt you."

"Can you do that? You've already taken enough risks for me."

"With the recording and another little investigation I've got going, trust me, the Harrisons'll be happy to leave town."

"But that's going to take at least until tomorrow. I'll have to find a motel."

The sheriff shook his head. "I want to make sure you're safe. You'll stay at my house; then it won't matter if Donald figures out where you are. That's what Tommy would have wanted."

"Okay."

"You know where the spare key is. Go on over there. The guest room is all made up. I'll be there inside an hour. I'll have a deputy follow you, so don't worry, there'll be no funny business."

She got up. "I don't know what I'd do without you."

He waved off her comment. "You would have figured it out on your own. But why bother if you don't have to? Have you ever turned me away when I needed help?"

"The help just seems all one way lately."

"I'll see you at the house."

The sheriff stood in the dark on the concrete steps in front of Harrisons' apartment, a heavy flashlight in his left hand, his right hand resting on the butt on his holstered pistol. He rapped on the door with the flashlight. The outside light came on and the door opened. George stood in the doorway, barefoot, dressed in blue sweatpants and a red long-sleeve T-shirt. "Sheriff," he said, taking a step back, "I didn't expect to see you."

"Why don't you invite me in?"

"Sure."

George stepped out of the way. Roslyn was sitting on the sofa, her feet on the coffee table. Her pink fleece robe was open over her sweatpants and T-shirt. When she saw the sheriff, she pulled her robe closed and turned off the TV. "Why are you here?"

"I'm concerned about your welfare."

She put her feet down. "How's that?"

George moved over by Roslyn and put his hand on her shoulder. "Hush up, Roz."

The sheriff shut the door and stood just inside the room, his hands down at his sides. "We're listening," George said.

"You're leaving town tonight. Disappearing. Never to be heard from again. Never to even drive through this county and stop for gas."

"Or?"

"I've heard the recording, which makes you part of a conspiracy to commit murder."

"That won't stand up. I gave the recording to Ms. Honeycutt."

The sheriff gave him a tired, bored look. "And while you're in jail waiting to make bail, I'll be getting a warrant to make casts of your tire treads, and we'll see if the cut marks on your tires match the casts we made at two county crime scenes."

158

"Can we get a few days to tie up loose ends? Roslyn's still a little weak to travel."

"Seems to me that riding in an Avalon is more comfortable than riding a cot in the county jail, but I guess some people don't know when law enforcement is going out of its way to help them out."

Roslyn looked up at George. "I'll be fine, Georgie. This place is nothing but bad memories. Let's just get out of here."

"Now you're talking," the sheriff said. "All this furniture is rent-to-own, isn't it? I'll call Franklin at the Rent-Today first thing in the morning, and he'll send his boys out to collect it." He opened the door to let himself out. "I expect you gone when I drive by here in the morning, or everything is going to be exactly by the book."

Billie sat on the side of the queen-size bed in the guest room of Bo Teardale's house. A picture of her ex in-laws, taken at the lake house up in Minnesota over twenty years ago, hung on the wall beside the closet. Her duffel bag sat open on the tan easy chair on the other side of the night table. Her toiletries bag was on the counter in the adjoining bathroom. She took her shoes off and sat back against the bamboo headboard. She had three phone calls to make. She called Jessup first. "Stan. I know it's late, but I've got an emergency."

"No problem, Ms. Honeycutt. I wouldn't have given you this number if I didn't want you to call."

"I'm going to need someone to stay at my house around the clock. Someone licensed to carry a gun. I'd prefer a woman."

"I've got a woman who fits the bill, but the problem is she's a single mom, so she can't stay all night. We could switch out at night; post someone outside if that works better for you. Have you been receiving threats of some kind?"

"I don't want to get into the details just yet. How old are her kids?"

"Teenagers. Two of them. She's trying to keep them on the straight and narrow. We could put a man on the front and the back doors. Nobody could get in."

"Let me think about it. I'll call back in a bit." She hung up the phone. Armed men at the front and back doors. That would certainly get the neighbors talking. Draw media attention. Who was she kidding? If she had Donald arrested, the reporters would be like paparazzi for the first few days. What to do?

She called Evelyn. "Evelyn, hope I didn't wake you."

"No, I was just going over our volunteer schedules."

"I've got some bad news."

"Involving the candidate? I thought the girlfriend miscarried."

"Worse."

"For Christ's sake, Billie, please tell me."

Billie told her about the recording.

"You're not kidding, are you? This isn't some bizarre misdirection stunt?"

"There's no doubt."

"Something to create so much confusion that no one will believe about the girlfriend?"

"I only wish."

"Because if there was any doubt—"

"The recording is absolutely chilling. When you hear it, you'll know."

The line went quiet. Billie thought maybe that the call had been dropped. "Hello? Evelyn?"

"I'm sorry, Billie. It's a lot to take in. My mind is churning. You must be devastated. What are you going to do now?"

"Well, the campaign's over."

"I'm not talking about the campaign. Of course that's flushed. The interns are going to be crushed. Truth be told, I didn't think it would survive the pregnant girlfriend. What are you going to do?"

"I'm still figuring it out. I haven't told Donald yet, but I couldn't stay in the house with him. I'm at Bo's for tonight."

"I have to say, Billie, I've known you and Donald a long time. I've worked with Donald on a lot of political projects. Don't get me wrong; I believe you, but the idea that he would hire someone to murder you—it's so crazy creepy. I mean, lots of handsome guys with charming personalities commit adultery—I'm not making excuses. That's just the way it is. So in my line of work, you just get used to it. But what you're saying? It's like I never even knew who he was."

160

"That's exactly it. That's why I couldn't stay in the house. He's a stranger. A stranger who tried to kill me. I've got no idea what he might do next. Beg forgiveness, plead temporary insanity, or smother me with a pillow in my sleep."

"You've got to think very carefully now. You don't want to underreact, but you don't want to overreact. You know what I mean. You want to keep your options open and close his off. If you want to talk—"

"Thanks. Do me a favor and don't break the news until I've thought things through."

"I don't want to pressure you, Billie, I mean, it's insane, but I can't wait too long. The interns deserve to know and I need to find a new job."

"I know." Billie hung up the phone. That went better than she thought it would. It was almost as if when Evelyn really considered it, she knew there was something wrong inside Donald that she just hadn't noticed before, but when it was brought up, made perfect sense. God, God, God, what would she do? What was the best way to protect herself? She called Jessup back.

"Stan. Your woman operative, what's her training?"

"Military police."

"Could she bring her kids? There's plenty of room."

"I could ask her. When do you want her?"

"Tomorrow afternoon."

"I'll be in touch in the morning."

"Thanks, Stan." She hung up. The last phone call she needed to make was to Donald, but she just couldn't bring herself to do it. She didn't want him to know that she knew he'd hired a killer, and she couldn't think of an excuse for why she wasn't coming home that would be believable. She padded into the kitchen and looked into the refrigerator. No yogurt, no celery, no baby carrots, no diet soda, only beer, lunch meat, cheese, and a wilted head of lettuce. She shut the door. Man food. But there was a bunch of bananas on the counter near the sink. She peeled a banana and took a bite. Her phone rang. She fished it out of her pocket. It was Donald. She didn't answer it. She walked through to the living room, eating her banana along the way. She saw Bo's headlights as he turned up the driveway in his sheriff's department cruiser. She heard the garage door go up. She felt safer already. She headed back to the kitchen.

The sheriff came in from the garage talking on his phone. "Yeah, I can't really go into it. This woman I know is going through a hard time. Billie's helping her. Yeah. She's staying over with her. Probably had it on vibrate." He put his phone in his pocket.

He looked at Billie. "That was Donald." He shrugged out of his sheriff's department jacket and laid it on the kitchen counter.

"Did he believe you?"

"Don't care." He got a can of beer out of the refrigerator. "Want one?"

She shook her head.

"I dealt with the Harrisons. Have you made a decision?" He opened his beer and took a drink.

She put the banana peel in the trashcan under the sink. "Yeah. Arrest him in the morning. That will give me time to change the bank accounts and talk with my lawyer."

"That's a lot of publicity."

"There'll be a lot of publicity anyway. This gives me the most time to set up my strategy to keep him from getting my money."

He set his beer on the counter. "I'm sorry about all this, Billie; I really am."

"It's not your fault."

13: Fallout

Honeycutt went into the bank early the next morning. He hadn't slept well and had woken up early; with Billie not home, he had no reason to hang around the house. At least he hadn't dreamed or couldn't remember the bad dreams he'd had. These last few days had been nightmare enough. It was as if he had woken out of a blissful fantasy of being a father and into an endless hangover where everything he'd once wanted no longer meant anything to him. The sun was shining. Green leaves were popping out on the bushes and trees. Birds sang and squirrels chased each other in circles. But for Honeycutt, the day was gray and empty. He was looking forward to a morning of endless paperwork, a noon meeting with a boring women's group, and an afternoon spent in the company of simpleminded volunteers at the campaign office. He hoped he'd get to see Billie before she left for Kansas City. He couldn't remember her telling him about that trip at all. He pulled into his parking space in the side lot next to the First National Bank. As he got out of his car, the sheriff pulled up behind him, blocking his car in.

"Hey, Donald, wait up."

Honeycutt turned. "Bo, is something up? Billie all right?"

"Yeah, she's fine." The sheriff strode over to him with his handcuffs in his hand. "You're under arrest, Donald."

"You got to be kidding."

"Turn around and put your hands on the car."

"Are you serious?"

The sheriff grabbed Honeycutt's shoulder and started to turn him, so Honeycutt did as he was told. "This can't be happening. My life can't get any worse. What's the charge?"

"Conspiracy to commit murder."

"Murder who?"

"Your wife."

"Are you insane? I can't claim to be the perfect husband, but I would never do anything to harm Billie."

The sheriff cuffed Honeycutt's wrists behind his back. "You're an excellent liar, Donald, but Harrison made a recording. Wonderful sound quality. So you can cut the bullshit." The sheriff led him to his cruiser.

"I need to speak to Billie."

"But she doesn't want to speak to you."

"This is all just a misunderstanding."

"Don't worry; you'll be out on bail before dinner." The sheriff opened the door to the backseat and helped Honeycutt get inside.

"This is what you've always wanted."

The sheriff shook his head. "Billie afraid for her life and made a fool of? No. I wish I had been wrong about you." He slammed the door to the backseat and climbed into the driver's seat.

"As soon as I talk to Billie, she'll make these charges go away."

The sheriff looked over his shoulder through the wire grate at Honeycutt. "If you go near her, so help me God, I'll see you and that Cadillac in Petersen's car crusher. You made your bed and now you're going to lie in it." He turned around and put the cruiser into drive.

After the sheriff called Billie to tell her that he'd arrested Honeycutt, she drove home. Mamie was at the kitchen sink hand washing a silver bowl when Billie came through from the garage. She could hear vacuuming upstairs. "Good morning, Mamie," she said.

"Good morning, ma'am. Where did you get off to so early?"

"I thought you had a doctor's appointment?"

"It was quick."

Billie sat down on a stool at the kitchen island and watched Mamie's back as she rinsed and dried the bowl. "I'm getting a divorce."

"Yes, ma'am."

"If Mr. Honeycutt comes in the house, call the police."

Mamie set the dried bowl on the counter near the sink and turned to Billie. She had a concerned mother's look on her face, but all she said was, "Coffee?"

"Please."

Mamie poured a cup and set in on the counter in front of Billie. Billie watched the steam rise off of the coffee, blew on it, and took a sip. Then she got out her phone. "Good morning, Evelyn."

"How are you doing, Billie?"

"Bo arrested Donald this morning. I still feel pretty crazy, but at least I feel safer."

"I put together a vague press release about Donald withdrawing from the campaign. I'm going to email it to the whole list."

"Great."

"I feel terrible for you. Your dreams smashed and your marriage. Unless you want to run yourself. You'd make a great candidate straight out of the box. Plus, you'd get the sympathy vote, at least in the primary."

"I've never been that interested in the nuts and bolts. I wanted to wheel and deal behind the scenes and let Donald hash out the details. Host some killer parties."

"You can always change your mind over the next few weeks."

"I'm not going to change my mind. I don't have the emotional and mental wherewithal to keep pushing forward. I'm completely empty."

"You'll get your mojo back, Billie. One day soon, you'll wake up in the morning and you'll feel like your old self again."

"I hope so. What's next for you?"

"I've got to put some feelers out to get on another campaign. It's still early enough."

"You're still on the payroll until the primary."

"Thanks. Money's not the issue. I need to be on somebody's team this cycle. I don't want to start over in two years."

"You'll find a spot, Evelyn. Good luck."

Billie set her phone on the counter. She sipped her coffee.

Mamie towel-dried some plastic containers out of the dishwasher. "So we're not moving to Washington, DC?"

"Not this year, Mamie."

In the late afternoon, after school, Cindi Butler drove over to Billie Honeycutt's house with her sons, James and Marcus. Jessup had insisted she go, and the overtime pay was twice her hourly rate, but she didn't really want to be there. She wanted to be off the job, at home, giving her boys her complete attention, not babysitting a rich woman who had nothing to fear. Besides, if Honeycutt did show up and she had to deal with him, she didn't want her boys to see that side of her. She wanted them to see her only as mom, not gun-in-hand, beating-down-the-perp mom. A Channel Six news van was parked on the street, as well as a Radio 1412 SUV, but the reporters weren't standing out on the sidewalk. They were probably expecting to follow a car rather than to actually catch a person of interest out in the yard. When Cindi pulled into the driveway in her blue Taurus, the news van flashed its headlights. She continued up the driveway, parked by the garage door and got out. James, almost six feet tall, dressed in jeans and a gray sweatshirt with the hood up, got out of the passenger's side. Marcus, a head shorter, wearing jeans and a red long-sleeve T-shirt with a school logo on the front, got out of the back. A blond reporter wearing a black skirt suit and a tan raincoat shouted at them from the sidewalk. "Who are you?"

Cindi, holstered gun hidden by her navy sports coat, glanced over her shoulder. "No comment."

"We going to get on TV?" Marcus asked.

James mimicked him. *"We going to get on TV?* Are you serious? Just listen to you."

Cindi looked sharply at her son. "Stop teasing your brother. I'm at work here."

"Uh-huh."

"Don't uh-huh me, boy. And pull that hood off."

They continued up the sidewalk to the front door. Cindi rang the doorbell. Mamie answered the door. "Come on in."

They stepped into the front hall. Mamie left them there. Marcus whispered, "That old white woman's wearing a maid uniform."

"Shush," Cindi said. "I told you these folks are not like folks you know."

Billie came out of the family room. She was wearing a gray scooped-neck T-shirt and red striped yoga pants with brown leather sandals. "Hi," she said, "I'm Billie Honeycutt." She stuck out her hand.

Cindi shook hands. "I'm Cindi Butler, one of Stan Jessup's associates, Ms. Honeycutt."

"I know who you are. Call me Billie. Everyone does except for Mamie."

"These are my sons, James and Marcus."

"Come on in, guys," Billie said. She started walking back toward the family room. "I'm so glad you could come, Cindi." She turned to the boys. "Guys, I want you to make yourselves right at home. We've got high-speed Internet. If you didn't bring a computer, I've got a couple of laptops lying around here. And we've got top of the line cable, if that's okay with your mom."

When they got into the family room, she motioned around. "Voila." She pointed into the kitchen. A tray of cheese and crackers, a bowl of chips, and a bowl of baby carrots sat out on the island counter. "There are soft drinks in the fridge. Please help yourselves."

Mamie stepped in from the front hall wearing her black coat. "If you don't need me anymore, ma'am, my ride is here."

"Thanks, Mamie, I'll see you tomorrow."

Mamie left. They heard the front door open and close. "Is anyone else here?" Cindi asked.

"Just us," Billie said. "I thought I'd order pizza after a bit."

"Thank you," Cindi said. She turned to her sons. "Why don't you two get started on your homework?"

Marcus sat down on a sofa and opened his backpack. "Can we eat in here?"

"Sure," Billie said.

James opened his backpack onto the dining room table, and then he went to the refrigerator and got a Coke. Cindi looked at the windows in the family room and the door that led to the garage. "I'm going to look at all the first floor access points." She went into the living room and looked at the windows there. Billie followed her. "Stan left things pretty open," she said. "Your security and peace of mind are our top priority. You've got quality locks, I assume you can alarm the downstairs separate from the upstairs, so I'm not quite sure why you need me overnight."

"I'm not concerned about a break-in. I'm concerned about my husband."

Cindi nodded. "I understand. Stan has another operative tailing your ex right now. If he comes here, we'll know. So really what we need to do is plan for the future. Do you know how to change the access code for the alarm?"

"The book is around here somewhere."

"Good. Have you got an alarm control pad in your bedroom?"

She nodded.

"It's too late today, but first thing tomorrow we'll call Greeley Security. They'll install a solid door with a reinforced lockset so you can use your bedroom as a panic room. The alarm kicks over downstairs. You lock yourself in the bedroom and call the police."

"Okay. But what about for the next few days?"

Cindi squeezed Billie's hand. "Everything is going to be all right. I'll stay as long as you need me, but the truth be told, your ex is more likely to beg or to run than to try to hurt you now."

The doorbell rang and the front door opened. "Billie?"

"That's Bo," Billie said.

"Me first," Cindi said. She led the way into the front hall, her hand casually on the butt of her holstered pistol. The sheriff was standing on the rug. "Sheriff Teardale," she said.

"You must be Cindi Butler."

"Yes, sir."

"Glad to see you on the job."

"I'll leave you two alone," Cindi said. She headed back toward the family room.

Billie got up on her tiptoes to give the sheriff a hug. "Come on in." She led him into the living room. They sat on the sofa. "Any news?"

"Donald made bail. Checked into the Holiday Inn. The DA says he'll press charges, but there isn't much hope. A recording by itself just isn't that convincing anymore. The mayor was almost gloating, but he got the chief of police to increase patrols by your house. So that's about it. You get the civil stuff done?"

"My lawyer got a restraining order. We're working on the divorce. I changed the bank accounts, so all he's got left is his own account. The locksmiths come to change the door locks tomorrow. Cindi says I should set up my bedroom at a panic room."

"Good advice."

"Evelyn put out a press release. She left the campaign."

"I heard about that. Chair of the County Commission wants Donald to resign."

She interlocked the fingers of her hands into a fist and put the fist up under her chin. "Somehow, it all just doesn't seem real. Right now, we should be planning our mopping up strategy for the primary. Instead, we're all done."

"Not forever. You could always run yourself."

"That's what Evelyn suggested."

"Smart woman."

She put her hands down and looked at him thoughtfully. "You've been a good friend to me."

"You'll always be my sister in-law, Billie."

"Have you ever thought about running for Congress?"

"Billie, I'm an old fashioned county official. I'd look as out of place as a mule at a racetrack. Besides, I love being sheriff. Why would I want to change?"

"Well, for one thing, you'd get me. I'd smooth everything out for you. It wouldn't take you long to update your moves."

"Billie, you should just run yourself if you have to have it. What are you afraid of? You could do it. Running yourself is no different from running Donald, except the candidate is more reliable. You'd win the primary easy." He stood up. "Quite frankly, the prospect of me and you being that close is just a little too strange. I like our relationship just the way it is."

She stood up as well. Her phone vibrated. She looked at it. Donald was calling. She didn't answer. She needed to get her phone number changed. "Why don't you stay for dinner?"

The sheriff shook his head. "I've got work to do. You're in good hands. You'll be fine. Call me if you need help."

14: Traveling

George and Roslyn sat on the queen-size bed in a spacious hotel room on Lakeshore Drive in Chicago, their backs against the padded leather headboard. They were still fully dressed, except for their shoes. He wore black pinstripe suit pants, a blue shirt, and a striped tie loose around his neck. She wore a loose, gold-colored three-quarter-sleeve dress with a pearl necklace. The TV was playing the late-evening news. The city noises — traffic and street activity — were a constant whisper through the closed windows. George squeezed Roslyn's hand. "What did you think of that restaurant?"

"I'd eat there again."

"Think we'll be here that long?"

"I'm in your hands, baby. What's the plan?"

"Sell the Avalon to a chop shop. Get you in to a gynecologist. Make sure your health is good."

"Then what?"

"Get the new passports and driver's licenses out of the Chicago lockbox."

She frowned. "You blew that last gig wide open. Gave up ten thousand a month at least until the election in the fall."

"Couldn't stand to be there anymore. Didn't like the way you were being treated." He patted her hand.

She took her hand away and rested it on her belly. "You ruined Donald's life."

"You don't really care, do you? That man ruined his own life. Look how he treated you. Look how he treated his wife. You can't cheat an honest man."

"People go crazy when they get the chance to have something they didn't even know they were missing."

He looked at her carefully. "Do you want another baby?"

She shook her head. "Too old. I don't know if I could stand it if something went wrong. It's just like, sometimes, you wish you had made different choices, ended up at a different place. It's not that the place you're at is bad, or doesn't have good stuff, it's just, you know, a feeling."

He put his arm around her and squeezed her shoulder. "Now you're making me feel old." He leaned over and kissed her. "But even though I'm old, and you've got your regrets, I'm going to make you so happy, starting right now, that ending up with me is going to be that different place you were trying to get to. Okay?"

"Okay."

He slid off the bed. "Do you want a glass of wine?"

"What kind?"

"We've still got a few bottles of the red you liked from the first house."

"How is that possible?"

"I saved them back."

"That was so sweet."

He got a bottle of wine out of a small roller bag in the bottom of the closet and went into the bathroom to get the wine opener out of his shaving kit. When he came back out, he carried two water glasses half-filled with red wine. He handed her a glass and crept back up on the bed, being careful not to spill his own. "Cheers."

They clinked glasses and drank. "So how much money do we have left?" she asked.

"Somewhere north of a hundred fifty thousand. Where would you like to go to spend it?"

"Cruise?"

He smiled. "You up for a cruise?"

"One of those Mediterranean cruises where you go to all the islands."

"Good food, interesting sights, retired rich folks looking for a good time. You talking work or pleasure?"

Her eyes brightened. "Maybe a little bit of both."

"That's my girl." He set his wine on the nightstand. "But my offer still stands, Roz. If you want out, we could use this opportunity to find you a rich husband."

"I don't want out. This is my life. Besides, I already have a rich husband."

He smiled. "You got that right. And our prospects just keep getting better." He glanced at Roz in the mirror on the closet door. She looked satisfied, relaxed, and happy, but he couldn't help but wonder just how much longer they'd be together.

A Note From the Author

Thanks for reading *The Blackmail Photos*. Please consider telling your friends or posting a short review on a review site of your choice. Your review will help other readers choose books that they'll enjoy.

I'd love to hear from you. You can reach me at my website: michaelpking.org.

The Travelers
The Traveling Man: Book One
The Computer Heist: Book Two
The Blackmail Photos: Book Three

www.ingramcontent.com/pod-product-compliance
Lightning Source LLC
Chambersburg PA
CBHW020126180626
46810CB00004B/1424